# A COPPER SNARE

Meet Detective Constable 'Randy' Jack Bull. Despite his nickname he is not happy with all the women in his life. Some of them are untrustworthy, some are mad — and some are dead. He also discovers that, as he watches his women, other people are watching him. Becoming increasingly bewildered by the case he is working on, and exhausted by overwork, he is all too easily ensnared by the melodramatic events that follow Carnival Night . . .

LAWRENCE WILLIAMS

# A COPPER SNARE

*Complete and Unabridged*

**LINFORD**
*Leicester*

First published in Great Britain

First Linford Edition
published 2006

This novel is entirely a work of fiction and no
reference to any real person, living or dead, is
intended.

British Library CIP Data

Williams, Lawrence, *1915 –*
    A copper snare.—Large print ed.—
Linford mystery library
1. Detective and mystery stories
2. Large type books
I. Title
823.9'14 [F]

ISBN 1–84617–526–7

Published by
F. A. Thorpe (Publishing)
Anstey, Leicestershire

Set by Words & Graphics Ltd.
Anstey, Leicestershire
Printed and bound in Great Britain by
T. J. International Ltd., Padstow, Cornwall

This book is printed on acid-free paper

*For police friends and acquaintances,*
*past and present, who have kept their*
*sense of humour.*

# Prologue

The red balloon drifted seaward over the rooftops. The watching crowd, eyes upturned like the dead, expelled a moaning breath: half-laugh, half-sigh. Presented with another balloon by his indulgent mother, the child uttered no thanks but stared round-eyed at the nearest adults. They had not seen what he had seen. Clutching the string of his new balloon he pushed his face into the warmth of his mother's thighs. He would not look up to the sky again in case that nasty man was still there.

The night of Carnival Procession should confirm the happy anticipations of the day; colour and noise, music and drink, laughter and fondling should fulfil all expectations. All the signs were favourable: hot day, fine evening; the flag-sellers, balloon boys, ice-cream men were busy; cheerful adults spilled out of the bars, grabbed at their offspring and

1

dragged them into the crowds at the roadsides. On the seafront, brass bands were unpacking, floats were being trimmed for the last time. The carnival queen and her ladies were shrugging out of their sensible woollies and simpering at the photographers. But almost submerged beneath the sights and sounds of carnival, other quite different preparations were being made.

For the past three years Clapton-on-Sea Carnival Week had been marred by the disappearance of a young woman. Each one had been reported missing the day after the carnival procession. Had a body been found the mutterings about 'the Yorkshire Ripper' or 'Boston Strangler' might have been justified. But there were no bodies. In the first two cases routine enquiries had been made and matters left to Missing Persons. It was the disappearance of the third girl that had raised the storm. The girl who vanished had been the Chief Constable's domestic help. Press and TV coverage had been considerable but once the British public had enjoyed a quick snigger the incident

2

was soon forgotten.

In Clapton itself, interest did not die so quickly. The locals enjoyed sharpening up remarks that passed for wit. Beat men were accosted and advised to raid their chief's attic or warned that their wives were getting suspicious about extra hours of night duty. Drivers of slow-cruising patrol cars were subjected to ribald advice about where to find the best pick-ups. Unfortunately, being bated by the vulgar-minded was not the only result of the girls' disappearances.

Sir Bertrand Slinfield, Chief Constable, imagined himself ridiculed in every factory, bus queue and pub in his county. He was quite right. He ordered interminable house to house searches, pond drainings, wood scourings and heath hunts. Extra men were drafted in from neighbouring forces, the Army supplied search teams, advisers came down from the Yard, and there was the usual rush of false alarms and of cranks with weird tip-offs. The result was absolutely nothing in terms of bodies but a great deal in terms of ill feelings, misunderstandings and bad temper.

The members of the county force, whilst complaining that Sir Bertie was taking things too personally, carried out all their extra duties. No one wasted breath pointing out that in all categories of crime their detection rate was above the national average. And with three nubile young women missing (disappearance added false glamour to lumpy, uninteresting females) it was unwise to boast of success with sexual offences. The only good result of all the extra work was that wife-beating ceased. A threatened spouse had only to utter a bleat and the whole police machine fell on her husband's neck.

As the year passed things had not returned to normal. The Chief Constable's bloody-mindedness was not forgiven by his men, and what he thought of as the failure of his Force became fixed in his mind as the failure of his own local station — and that was Clapton-on-Sea. In the Spring he had demanded that the carnival be cancelled. Other views prevailed. The effect on public relations would have been disastrous. Local businessmen would have complained of lost profits, and so public a confession of inadequacy would have seriously damaged public confidence in the police. It was also pointed out, by a brave senior officer near retiring age, that the Chief Constable was laying himself open to more personal criticism on the grounds that no such action had been taken when other people's *au pair* girls had disappeared. This argument had carried some weight. In addition, there was still no specific evidence that a crime had been committed or that another girl might choose to disappear on carnival night.

Carnival week had begun in an atmosphere of ghoulish anticipation. Local and national newsmen had been working in the town, stirring up doubts and fears, making their own news for the silly season. TV coverage of the procession had been arranged for the first time. All the media were gathered together and the Chief Constable made sure he was in the midst of them. He had set up the biggest and most highly publicized security operation ever mounted in his county.

The inhabitants of Clapton-on-Sea had responded by raising the price of ice-cream, choosing the bustiest carnival queen they could find, providing more and better floats, and engaging five bands instead of three to play in the procession. No one mentioned the reason why Cancer Research and the Old Folks Home would receive record donations this year. For the same reason every bed and breakfast could have been sold three times over. And even the plainest and most acned girls in local youth clubs had been paired with an unwilling male escort for the evening. Rumour is never an ill-wind.

# 1

Despite what judges have said I am not really a violent man but I could cheerfully have murdered that child. As his bloody balloon bobbed up in front of me I flattened myself behind the parapet and two sharp pieces of roofing gravel nipped my right ball. As I bounced up again in agony some of the crowd may have seen me but I was past caring. Knackered in more senses than one I collapsed and nursed my several grievances.

The flat roof had been sunstruck all day. (No wonder Cloag had smirked when announcing dispositions.) I had been lying there for over an hour slowly sinking into the blistering bitumen while those sodding gravel chippings sank into me. Of course, all my colleagues were hidden on shaded rooftops or sitting in armchairs at the curtained windows of cool rooms.

I did not want to think of my own cool room. A white, secret room where, lying in bed listening to soft lapping waves in the harbour, I can see their rippling lights reflected on the ceiling. And there is a well-stocked fridge. I heard a rasping noise, realized I was licking parched lips. But there was a far bigger agony in thoughts of that room. The room was inseparable from remembrance of Jeannie. She was gone. I remained.

A shrink might have said my anger was about Jeannie but he'd only be half-right. There was plenty of anger left over for this crazy case. Young women don't vanish for one, two or three years except willing — or dead. And there had been no 'don't worry' notes. The unwilling should turn up in shallow graves, or float bloated and stinking onto the beach. They had not done either of those things so for most people there was no cause for alarm. But I had a nasty feeling about those girls.

Some of my anger was caused by

suspicion that the piss was being taken. A mad hatter was repeating the same crime once a year, and in case we hadn't got the message he'd taken Sir Bertie's girl last time. The rest of my anger came from a feeling of helplessness. How could so few men keep watch over a population almost doubled by the influx of holidaymakers? We had fallen back into familiar routines that could not begin to meet a new situation. No amount of high-sounding language from a Chief Constable could disguise that fact.

A maroon thudded. Gulls rose shrieking from the harbour. The first band struck up. The waiting crowds began to shuffle and people near the start of the procession route began to cheer. I switched on my radio. At headquarters the spools of tape began to turn, waiting to trap any word spoken by any watcher. At the edge of town traffic police blocked off every exit. Miles away, unknown colleagues in other counties sealed off their boundaries with us. The traps were closed. High above the harbour a red balloon burst.

# 2

Saturday, 20.00–20.30 Hrs

Suddenly, the crowd heaved and quivered, heads swivelled in unison to catch first sight of the procession. Excitement rose as the clashing bands drew nearer, as the froth of cheering washed slowly from the Promenade along the High toward Cross Street. Feet tapped to the rising music, hands began to clap the rhythm. Idiot children surrendered more balloons to drift in the faces of the yakking gulls. I focused my glasses on the far end of Cross Street. The crowd ejaculated a harsh shout that hurt my head.

The police car leading the procession edged round the corner as if fearing a trap. It entered my binoculars and sprang up to rooftop height. The driver and observer stared ahead.

'Tango Seven here,' I said. 'Procession entering Cross Street now. PCs Jones and

Piper are leading. No sign of the Revellers yet.'

The town band stamped into view, all gilt buttons and red braid, peaked caps already climbing back off their sweaty heads. They were the first of five bands and meant to show us why. Their music, funnelled in the straight street, came ripping between the facing ranks of the crowd.

Police car and band were suddenly absorbed into a riotously coloured background of flowers, ferns and posters as the prize-winning first float rounded the corner. Giant-headed pierrots and masked dancers burst out from behind the float, began dancing and spinning in the gutters, waving collecting boxes, diving into the crowd for money or to haul out a willing partner for the dance. Giggling girls were ransomed for cash or kisses. Children broke from parents and scuttled into the road like mice. The front ranks of the crowd mingled with the procession. The crowd became the carnival.

As the procession advanced toward me it was the crowd I watched, moving my glasses from pavement to pavement looking for — what? After all the theorizing, all the briefings, I knew only that I was looking for any strange incident involving a girl. Perhaps she was being dragged into a doorway against her will or led out of the crowd for no reason. But how often girls were being kissed in door-ways, offering token resistance as part of the game. How often girls were being led into the road to dance. Hopeless to watch all these incidents.

Figures in the procession were also watching. Staggering on human legs, a ten-feet high Humpty-Dumpty turned cold eyes left and right as it wobbled past. Poor old PC Buttle would never live it down. There were worse places than my roof. But where were the Revellers? They usually led the procession by jumping in ahead of it somewhere along the route.

From an alley leading obliquely into Cross Street spiky black shadows sprang over the crowd and crawled up the stuccoed wall opposite. From the throat of the alley burst a tall hollow-faced squinting man dressed in the tattered uniform of a French drummer at Waterloo. It was Art Greening, petty crook. He glanced at the procession bearing down on him from his left and began to beat a harsh staccato rhythm on his drum. The signal was answered.

Out of the alley trundled Granny Hemyock, pushed in her wheelchair by Greening's inseparable companion Snoad. Dressed as an eighteenth-century footman in a nasty acid yellow material, Snoad bowed himself over the chair as he struggled to steer a course not dictated by the wild movements of his passenger. His bald head glistened with sweat, his face puckered as if he was on the point of tears. He ducked as Granny took a wild swing at the crowd with her placard. Fortunately, everyone had stepped aside to let her out of the alley. Her placard bore the legend 'Revellers' crudely painted in red on black. In her black cape, with black pointed hat above scowling face, she was no figure of fun but a creature who silenced children as she lurched past. More gullible adults assumed that the curses she mouthed were good wishes for their enjoyment of the carnival.

Snoad and Granny were followed by a tall figure in a blood-red hood and cape. The hood slits revealed glittering eyes probing at the crowd. He carried a pitchfork on which was spitted a skinned rabbit. I felt a kind of sick excitement but I did not know who it was. After him came a brawny transvestite in short skirts, puffed sleeve blouse, wrinkled tights and with his face heavily rouged. His muscular arms and hands, heavily tattooed, were a ludicrous contrast to his costume. He should have been a figure of vulgar fun but somehow, in that company, he was disgusting. 'Joe Block!' I snarled at my radio. Lastly, came a slim, dreamy-eyed blonde girl strewing herbs and grasses in the path of the procession. She walked just ahead of the police car taking care not to throw her herbs onto the bonnet; the only sign she was aware of her surroundings. She was Granny's great-niece, a registered addict, and the foulest mouth I've ever heard. She walked so slowly, so deliberately, she soon forced open a gap between

Granny's chair and the police car.

That group was a small, festering sore in Clapton; a gang of layabouts, perverts and petty crooks. Had they been big time I might have regarded them differently. But the only one of Granny's associates with a substantial mark against him was Pete Rymer, 'The Carver'. But he was not in the party; he was too short to be the man under the red hood. But never mind Rymer. My job was checking on people I could see.

Greening now beat his drum in time with the leading band. He marched beside Granny. The red-hooded figure also came close, bowed over her, spoke. Granny stopped waving, hesitated, then shook her head. The hooded figure leaned still closer and Granny pointed upward at my position. I felt as if a skewer had been driven through me. She was ninety feet away and it seemed ninety inches. I ceased breathing, lay rigidly still. Then her minions closed in and began a slow ungainly dance round the moving chair. With a careless gesture the girl flicked herbs at the crowd. I began to breathe again.

I watched them until they had passed round the corner and out of sight. I took a quick look back along Cross Street: nothing obviously wrong there. I scrambled across the roof and looked down into the next street. The Revellers had advanced about forty yards from the corner. The six figures were dancing much faster, bobbing and swaying round the loaded chair which was freewheeling down the slight slope. Then the police car also turned the corner and began to close up behind them. As the full force of the band struck up in my face I crawled back to my original position looking down on Cross Street. The street was now jammed with floats, two more bands, groups of dancers in fancy dress, and the bubbling roaring crowd. The noises, movements, colours made my head swim. I was doubly glad to screw my binoculars tight into the Carnival Queen's splendid bust.

# 3

Half an hour later the tail of the procession lurched past. In its wake great sections of the crowd broke from the pavements and drifted down the street like pack ice in a cleared channel. Suddenly, Cross Street was quiet and cool. I stood up, massaged cramped limbs; evening was cooling the sweat. Pulling on my jacket I looked across a forest of spires, towers, chimney stacks and roofs. Above was a sky of palest green and lemon. Between roofs to the left a broad tract of silver sea was already being gilded by the rising moon. Just for a moment it was my town again. Almost reluctantly, I radioed my departure. Squelching across the roof, I looked back at the depression made by my body and enjoyed the thought that someone was going to get wet next time it rained.

Someone ought to share my discomforts.

Standing on the bottom step of the fire escape I looked along Cross Street. Dusk and shadow did not hide the mess the crowd had left: plastic cups, streamers, newspapers, bottles, even some dead fish thrown by a gang of pirates on one of the floats. As I stepped into the road my foot caught against something solid. I picked up a toy pistol, a realistic model in heavy black plastic: Smith and Wesson .38 Special, about two-thirds real size. It could prove a dangerous toy. I put it in my pocket.

Walking along the darkening street I saw a man stooping in doorways, checking locks.

''Lo, Dan. What you doing?' I asked, foolishly.

'Evenin', Jack. Just checking, here and there.'

Detective Sergeant Dan Thirkettle, CID, my immediate superior and checking door knobs! If, the big if, I ever stagger to that exalted rank I'll not be checking door knobs. Or will I? What does endless exhaustion do to a man? Knowing myself to be older than the granite kerb-stone I could not stifle all sympathy for Dan, twenty years longer under the hammer. And for what? Insults in court from clever briefs, indifference from the public, an ulcer to nurse in retirement? Aren't our policemen wonderful? Whenever there is some shitty complaint against us it is always Dan's tired face that comes to mind. And now I didn't know what to say to the man.

'Er — reckon we're wasting our time again, Dan. Trying to do the impossible tonight, aren't we?'

'There's no other way, lad. Someone's gonna try and watch over the public. You've seen nothin' unusual?'

'No. Same as last year.'

'I didn't see the Revellers in the High.'

'They picked up the procession here in Cross Street. Sod 'em!'

'Aye, lad. Petty crooks showing off on a night out. Trying to make a point: two fingers.' A long silence. Something about Dan went further than exhaustion. How many old CID men went slightly mad; not certifiable, just a kind of mental dislocation?

'On the other hand,' I said, awkwardly, 'having Granny and her mob in the limelight means we know what they're up to.'

'Yes, lad. But they're small fry anyway. We're looking for something far bigger.'

'But what?'

'Well, the first girl to go worked for that Colonel Tremayne, didn't she?'

'You think we should go back to the start?'

'Where else can we go? And Tremayne's got influence, money, business contacts, etc. He's heavily involved with a construction company isn't he? That gives opportunities to bury bodies.'

'But we checked all the building sites last year. You had a whisper, Dan?'

'No, Jack. Just thinking aloud. How about you?'

'Not a bloody word.'

'That ain't your fault, lad.'

'Maybe not.' Another silence. 'I'll move on, Dan. Bit chilly after all that sun. Pity we can't turn in now.'

'Hmm. You got the sea end of the High and part of the Prom.'

'Yes. Until midnight.'

'At least you ain't on all night. And we're not stuck out at the roadblocks either.'

'You guessing another girl'll disappear, Dan?'

'God knows. If it happens again all we can say is we did what we could with the men we've got. Supposed to have help down from London y'know. No sign of it.'

'Could be lying low.'

'Why d'you say that?' Dan's voice was shrill.

'Dunno. Just a thought.' His jumpiness alarmed me. 'Suppose I'm bothered we've not had a whisper in three years. Small town, you and me with reliable grasses, and we've got sod all to show.' But I was making things worse.

'What's that got to do with lyin' low? Do they think no squeak means police corruption?'

'Take it easy, Dan! I'm only supposing. It's just that when there's no flow of information you can't be surprised if someone suspects a kink in the pipeline.'

'That's pitchin' it strong, lad — and putting it on the likes of us. We don't need anything else putting on us, do we?'

'Christ, Dan! If another bird vanishes and we still get nothing we'll be bloody put on all right. The least that'll happen'll be a rash of transfers and more blocked promotions. D'you want to be moved out of Clapton? Neither do I. All my roots are here.'

'That might be another of your mistakes, Jack. You need a move.' I was not sure he meant it kindly. 'You're young enough to make a fresh start.'

'Could be.' Try humour, try anything. 'It could be we've not met the Yard team because someone thinks it's you or me making off with the birds.'

'You know me and my missus well enough to realize all the suspicion'll fall on you, Randy Jack Bull.' Dan smiled mirthlessly. 'Night, lad.' I was left to take myself to the water's edge, presumably to jump in.

The seaward end of the High was jammed with the remnants of procession and crowd. Each of the parked floats had turned into a kerbside bar and crates of beer were being dragged out from under the decorations. The scout float appeared to be the only exception but some of the boys looked both unsteady and unready. No matter. Let joy be unconfined for as long as there was no missing person report. Recognizing the harmlessness of the bribe, I accepted the can of beer shoved at me by old Mr Futcher, driver of the scout float. Then I walked slowly along the seafront.

The coloured lights of the Promenade and its hotels shed a soft glow on the beach where lovers, townsfolk and holi-dayfolk, were grappling onto each other under the starlit sky. And that Walt Disney moon over the sea. I thought of all the springtime babies being made that night. 'Randy — you're nasty!' As I drained the beer can, old Mrs Dazley crept past showing the whites of her eyes as she fell thankfully down the steps of the nearest beer cellar. I hadn't meant to speak aloud. Better keep moving. CID must show uniformed branch an example. And there was always the chance the sneaky Inspector Cloag was out looking.

Walking toward the old harbour, its cottages turned backside toward the town, I came to the Drum public house.

Outside, on the quay, was the local climax to carnival night. The Salvation Army band was playing to the crowd; the coloured lights reflected in their silver instruments. Laughter burst from the pub. There were smells of warm beer, of cockles and vinegar, of hot dogs and fried onions. All this beneath the gold and silver sprays of the Town Park firework display shooting over the rooftops and climbing up against the night sky.

Almost enjoying the brilliant scene I felt a coldness across my neck, as if a gentle night breeze came off the sea. Was I being watched? I stood still, tired brain struggling with possibilities. Was it Cloag, Dan, strangers? I turned quickly and was confronted by the horrified stare of a small child clutching a balloon. Perhaps it was my abrupt movement that distressed the child. It burst into tears and ran back to its mother. I turned back to the band knowing it was not the child who spied. Walking slowly into the middle of the road, turning again, I saw the eyes gleaming in the alley. Whoever was watching stepped back into the dark shadow. I walked swiftly into the alley, heard running feet ahead, began to run. A burst of fire-works threw down enough light for me to glimpse the figure ahead. I was chasing someone in skirts.

At the end of the alley I skidded into a quiet square at the rear of the seafront hotels. Nothing moved but I did not suppose I was alone. Nervously, I turned my back on the square and walked briskly into the safe warmth and vivacity of the crowd. If someone chose to watch — well. And what would I report? Attempted to arrest someone, sex unknown, with a view to charging him/her with police watching? Yes, sir, I had been drinking just before the incident. Yes, a single pint on top of fifty hours overtime might have an unexpectedly severe effect. Yes, I would normally know the difference between a man and a woman. As you say, sir, my reputation as a womanizer.

But why run away? Very slowly I walked along the seafront. Was it a woman? On this one night of the year it could have been a man in carnival costume, perhaps in a blood-red cloak and hood.

# 4

Sunday, 06.30–09.30 Hrs

I woke from dreams of female bodies
lacerated by hooded fiends, broken in
ghastly rituals; had recognized most of
the victims. With eyes tight shut I lay
gasping in knotted sheets. Eventually, I
forced open my eyes and saw light
rippling on a familiar ceiling. Thankfully,
I stretched out in the huge dishevelled
bed, smoothed away the cramps of those
dreams. Some time later I groped for my
watch. 06.30 hours, Sunday morning. No
great hurry, not due to report until 10.00.
Dull routine awaited me, checking print-
outs, reports, writing my own report.
Thought of writing a report revitalized
the feelings of alarm that had moved in
me twice last night. I had a visit to make
before reporting for duty.

I lurched from my bed, switched off the
unnecessary alarm clock, stumbled over

clothes I had been too exhausted to hang up last night. I shaved, cutting myself, then took a long shower: hot, cold, hot again; felt some of the leaden tiredness wash away leaving just the exhausted core. I towelled slowly, shrugged into my silk dressing-gown, padded into the kitchen, prepared toast and coffee, inhaled the fragrance while looking out across the harbour from the first-floor window. No fishing boats rode out today. The calm sea stayed unruffled while fishermen slept off the effects of carnival night. I put the coffee pot, cream jug, breakfast cup and saucer on a tray; added the plateful of thick toast, butter dish and jar of favourite coarse cut marmalade. I unlocked the outer door of the kitchen, picked up the tray and backed out against the door onto the small roof garden overlooking the harbour quay. It was already a very hot day. I lay back on the lounger; present from a grateful young lady. I sipped coffee, stared at the sea.

I started every day as early as possible. Early rising was a way of making a break between sleep and the crushing workloads of the past few weeks. There was a second reason: not bearing the bed when awake. The procession of bewildered pick-ups who had shared my nights since Jeannie did nothing to diminish my dread of the haunting, remembering early mornings.

I poured another cup of coffee, spread butter and marmalade on toast, and wondered how much longer I would survive.

At 09.00 hours I knocked on the side door of number ten, King Street: Arthur Gross, Modern Modes. Only the initials were correct. I heard the faint scraping of wood against wood, knew the spyhole was open. A chain rattled, bolts were drawn.

'Please come in, Mr Bull.'

'Thank you, Judith.' The hall was ill-lit but I knew her dark troubling loveliness well enough. I followed along the greasy tunnel of hallway, past the heavily barred door leading to the second-hand clothing shop, and on towards the brighter light of a distant room.

'Abraham,' she said, happily, 'it is our friend Mr Bull.'

'Mr Bulls. Welcome. Please be seated.' The frail figure of Abraham Gretz gestured towards a chair at the opposite side of the dining-room table. As I sat down my right hand was grasped by both hands of the little Jew. 'You come on your Sabbath, not mine.' The dry coughing chuckle was recognition not of his own joke but of a well-worn ritual. I nodded. I now had a choice of two responses.

'I've come for a little chat, Abe.'

'Indeed.' The goatee beard jerked upward, the eyes were hard. 'Judith you will please make coffee.' She inclined her head, dark hair sweeping forward onto the curving ledge of her breast. Abraham waited until she had left the room.

'What can I do for you, Mr Bulls?'

'Got anything for me, Abe?'

The old bright eyes glittered in the dark face, acknowledging the contempt behind the crude abbreviation of his name. But he understood policemen so very well, had long lived with the conflicts between friendship and the distaste for an informer, between independence and gratitude.

'Nothing new. If I had urgent information you know that after what you did for my Judith — '

'Yes. Let's forget that.' But the old man would not be deflected. Observance of rituals is protective. Ask any Jew. Or policeman.

'But there were three of them — and one with a knife. You saved her for me.' The trace of maliciousness behind the last phrase was also part of the ritual. I had rescued the girl from three drunken young thugs and had enjoyed hopes of saving her heavy-breasted, thick-hipped beauty for myself. Chagrin on discovering the old 'grandfather' was actually her lover had been impossible to hide from the keen eyes now watching me. But I had won the eyes. Abraham was the sharpest, the best of grasses. And his second-hand clothing trade took him everywhere.

'You sure there's nothing new?'

'Strangers in your town.'

'Bloody'ell! It's the middle of the holiday season. What else do — '

'No, Mr Bulls. Official strangers. Wait!'

Judith entered carrying a small copper tray, jug of bitter coffee, tiny cups, cream.

'Thank you, my dove,' said Abraham,

touching her thigh. Gravely, she bowed, found space between his thick eyebrows and greasy white hair to plant a demure kiss. I suppressed a shudder. When she had left the room, closing the door behind her, Abraham poured coffee.

'Official strangers,' he repeated. 'Of your police force.' I felt sick. What had I said to Dan? 'One a very large man with little hair — I mean hair cut very short. Saw him leaving your police station. Your Mr Shalvin was being so very polite.'

'You said strangers?'

'The big man had another man to drive him. Not a uniform man.'

'Are they still in town?'

'Have not seen them. But as you say — with all the holiday peoples — ' The shrug, the arm movements unchanged since the first Abraham.

'When did you see them?' I asked, irritably.

'Last Wednesday, first day of carnival week. But not since.'

We sipped coffee, busy with very different thoughts.

'And the girls?' I asked, at last. 'Any

news about girls missing?'

'Your police have lost *another* one?' Abraham's straight face was enough to make me chuckle. Relieved, Abraham smiled as well, wrinkled face crinkling like soiled tissue paper.

'Not that we've heard. But after the last three — '

'No news has come to me. But then it did not come to me on the other times.'

'How can the bloody business be kept secret?' I banged my fist on the table.

'Strange, Mr Bulls. That one question you never asked me before.'

'No?'

'No. You ask about particular people, about facts, about particular crimes, but never before have you asked that question — '

'And now you're going to tell me?'

'You will not be pleased. So many answers, so many circumstances are possible here.'

'Try me, Abe. Anything. We've got no answers.' I was dangerously close to pleading — and with a grass!

Abraham refilled the coffee cups. He

32

took his coffee black. The cream was for my weaker palate. 'I can speak my experiences if you wish it.' The old man was holding his cup very tightly. I nodded. I knew of the tattoo on his wrist.

'One sort of secret is that there is no secret.'

'You mean the girls disappeared of their own free will? It's just coincidence it was carnival night each time?'

'Maybe that is so. There is another way.' Abraham sipped coffee. 'I know it. The way of all knowing.'

'What's that supposed to mean?'

'If enough people know the secret they would all know not to speak of it.' He raised a hand warding off gentile irritability. 'Do you really believe the German people did not know about the camps? That six millions of us died and only the camp guards knew? They *all* knew so did not speak of it, came to believe, to shelter, in their own assumed cloak of ignorance.'

'But in this small town?'

'Mr Bulls, some of the camps were small towns. And if a whole nation can live with six million dead *anything* is a possibility.' I was silenced. Not even born when the millions died how could I oppose the man's experience with mere probabilities.

'There are other ways of secrecy. Ways as bad. What I tell you now no one else must ever know, especially not my Judith.' The man's voice was changing to a kind of whining sing-song. He rocked from side to side on his chair.

'Of course,' I said, dry-mouthed.

'When they — the guards took me out of the line I did not at first understand it was my youth, my strength that saved me. They needed some of us to bury the others, you understand? The first bodies I dragged out of the gas chambers, carted to the pits, included my mother. Then I had to watch and wait while her gold fillings were torn out. I said nothing, did nothing. If I had betrayed myself by my mother's naked body imagine the things those animals might have done — made me do. There is that sort of secret keeping, Mr Bulls.' Abraham stared into his cup. 'But I tell you more. The man who took out the teeth was still at the camp at the war's end, three years later. I did not let him escape. A Jew from Smyrna knows much of what history teaches of tortures. I will not tell you how I made him die but in his agonies *then* he learnt of my secret. The true revelation eh? I did not kill him quickly, Mr Bulls. He would have preferred the gas chambers.'

'Someone like that here — here in Clapton?' I said, weakly.

'Why not? *I* am here. You ask of three girls, three years. I kept *my* secret three years. I am not mad now, not cruel, not young. You could say of me I am ordinary. Perhaps some other man or woman like me, like a guard — '

'So one minute you suggest a crowd, the next a suffering, secretive individual.'

'So now I make it worse for you. Why not a cell? Like communists, eh? Little group, meeting in secret, disguised from each other, equally guilty. Like a — like a — '

'Like a gang-bang?' I was deliberately crude.

'Ye-es. I think that is what I mean. But not knowing their leader. Or if knowing then held by blackmail, fear. Imagine their minds if they have used three victims already. How can they stop it now?'

'Christ!'

'Eh?' The old man banged his cup on the tray. 'No help to you.' It was not clear whether he meant Christ or himself. 'If any news comes to me you know I will — '

'Yes, yes. Thank you, Abraham.' I was anxious to escape. 'You can phone me: usual number, usual names.'

'You are late now for work?' asked the old man, spitefully. It was not only Germans who had not wanted to know. 'Judith! Judith, come and see our visitor to the door. At least you have one new idea, Mr Bulls. Someone strange has been with your police. Of all men in this town *I* know the official persons, with or without uniforms. They have a smell I do not forget. Like with the dying, you know?'

# 5

I wandered slowly along the beach. The tide was in along with driftwood, polythene bottles, paper wrappers and cigarette stubs. Perhaps the flotsam was physical representation of my state of mind; so many ideas aground on lack of evidence. Gretz had probably spoken the truth somewhere in all that he had said. But where? He and I and Dan Thirkettle each knew Clapton as well as one could know a town and its people. Yet all we had after three years were theories. All the searches, whispers, silences had left us stranded. It was disgusting but understandable that some of my colleagues were half-hoping for another disappearance. It would at least confirm we were dealing with crimes.

At 09.45 I arrived at the station. The air of neglect that usually characterized the place on Sundays was replaced by the bustle of a weekday just before the Bench sat. Clapton-on-Sea was temporarily County HQ.

Sergeants Bradninch and Bone were behind the desk together like uniformed impersonations of Laurel and Hardy. I winced at the thought of what Bone must be suffering working with that fat slob.

'Morning, Sergeant Bone.'

'Mornin', Jack. Quiet around town?'

'Real hung-over place it is. Like walking in a graveyard. Everyone wincing at the thought of breakfast.'

'Sufferin' for a good night last night. Enjoy the procession?'

'Oh, sure. Stuck up on that bloody roof! No bad news this year, Sarge?'

'Not so far, Jack. Not so far.' Bone would certainly know of the mildest whisper coming in.

But our conversation had gone on too long for Bradninch. He was not going to be ignored. He pressed his huge stomach against the desk, leaned forward to peer affectedly into my face. I stared back while the tiny dinosaur brain ground its way toward a humorous remark.

'Why, it's Detective Constable Randy Jack Bull. Look Bone, it's our chief suspect out of bed early on a Sunday. Very suspicious. Where's yer latest woman, Randy?'

Why bother to reply. The man disgusted me. The masses of fat that clung to his frame were the swollen inheritance of a former career as hammer thrower. Selected for the Olympic squad long, long ago he had, on his day, performed as a true British sportsman by failing to qualify for the finals. How he had *nearly* made the final was one of his two topics of conversation. Olympic selection and promotion to sergeant had come in the same year. Now he was truly stuck. Not even an unhealthy, persisting interest in child molesters (his other topic of conversation) could earn him elevation.

'She suck yer tongue out, then?'

Leaning across the desk, I stared into his bulging face. 'You disgust me beyond words. That's why I'm bloody silent!'

'Hey! I don't have to put up with — '

'Don't bother, Sarge. I'll deny it.'

Angrily, I turned away. I'd let the slob get to me. Bone's raised eyebrows didn't help. Bradninch turned toward him and the eyebrows fell but Bradninch was going to make his point anyway.

In the CID room was Detective Chief Superintendent Shalvin, Head of County CID.

'Morning, sir.'

'Good morning, Bull. Shut the door. That fool Bradninch is shouting again. Been needling him?'

'Certainly not, sir.' Neither of us smiled.

'I want you to check these reports and transcripts of the recordings made last night.'

'Anything special, sir?'

'No, not yet. But you know what'll happen if we get a missing person report this time. So we're going to be a jump ahead or, at least, in the starting blocks.'

'Yes, sir. All the routine done.'

'No, Jack. All the routine done with exceptional thoroughness. I'm not having anyone pick on CID if the crunch comes.' The telephone rang. Shalvin grabbed it.

'Yes, he's here. For you, Bull, a Mr Smithson.'

'DC Bull here. Hello, Abe. This is quick.' I faced away from Shalvin. 'I was *what*?

'Sure?

'Description?

'What d'you mean by that? Was he on a horse?'

'Yes, clever. I know the picture *and* get the picture. Is that all? And to you, mate.'

I slammed down the phone. Shalvin looked at me hard.

'Sorry, sir. An informant.'

'So I assume. What was the bit about a horse?'

'Some damn-fool description about a man looking like the Duke of Wellington, that painting by Goya.' Shalvin looked blank. 'Might as well've been Napoleon. Said he kept one hand in his pocket.'

Suddenly, Shalvin's blank expression was frozen. A connection had been made but it by-passed me.

'Er — I was saying, Jack,' Shalvin was now shifty, 'what I want is — I want Sir Bertie left in no doubt that we did all we

41

could to avert disaster. If you find anything, anything that doesn't add up we'll follow up at once. Use that ruddy nose of yours. See if anything's been missed.'

'Right, sir.' I didn't resent remarks about my nose. Shalvin was experienced enough to believe in a sixth sense for trouble. It was the pushy middle ranks, the whizz kids and Bramhill fliers, promoted too fast, who did not believe. 'Much to clear up from last night, sir?'

'No, not for us. But the traffic boys had a good time. They got thirty-eight on the breathbag, three stolen cars and about twenty tax and insurance dodgers.'

'Christ! You'd think with all the fuss, all the publicity about our plans, the silly buggers'd've been more careful.'

'You know how thick the brethren can be. Anyhow, that's not our problem. I'm going back to Harmsworth now. Cloag'll be looking in on you about 14.00.'

'Right. Thank you, sir.' Thanks were for the warning that Inspector Cloag would be on the prowl. No other thanks were due. Shalvin was excluding me from his confidence as far as strangers were concerned, but he had slipped up slightly when I mentioned a man with hand stuck in pocket. Gretz had telephoned I'd been tailed from King Street and Shalvin had recognized that part of the description. As a mere detective constable there was no point in trying to force the issue — yet. A more immediate worry was my own failure to detect the tail — and in almost deserted streets. I was either too damned tired or dealing with a top pro.

I concentrated on the reports, almost welcomed drudgery, was scarcely aware of any life outside the CID room. Later, someone brought tea and biscuits. I drank the tea when it was cold, ignored the biscuits. When the first part of the job was complete I was sure that, if all the reports were accurate, no young woman had been abducted by car or coach. There were other checks to make but I was fairly confident that if anyone had vanished they had either gone by sea or were still in the town. Interrupted by Detective Inspector Cloag at 13.50 hours, I stated these conclusions. Cloag leered, fingered his Hitler moustache, murmured it might be wise to check the sea route.

'Just about to do so. Instead of lunch, sir.' Cloag, smiling sweetly at his little victory, retired to fawn upon the Chief Constable. 'Prick!' I said, marching out to wrest the coastguard reports from Sergeant Bradninch.

By mid-afternoon I was putting my money on the fact that no one had left town unwillingly. No boat had sailed, no roadblock had been forced, no cross-country route employed. There were no anomalies between all the different reports and the station books. No policeman had arrested a drunk and lost her on the way to the station. There had been exactly the right number of found children to return to exactly the right number of distraught parents. It was clear that just about every possible emergency had been covered by the Chief Constable's planning. What was wrong was what was always wrong. Meticulously organized operations can only be designed for foreseeable emergencies. That was a point I had not written into my own report. It would be as unwelcome as any reference to chasing skirted figures up alleys.

Despairing, I compared what I had written with the other reports covering the same part of the procession route. For the first time I noticed a slight discrepancy but doubted if it was significant. I was the only observer in the vicinity of Cross Street who had not seen Pete Rymer. Perhaps that proved I was the doziest man on duty. It was unlikely to prove much else. Rymer was very tightly in my pocket.

PC Buttle had almost nothing to report, had written a model report of nothing to report. How could a man dressed as a giant Humpty Dumpty describe his ridiculous wobbling progress in the words: 'I proceeded . . . '? On the other hand his superiors would not have been pleased to read that he had wobbled in Cross Street. But PC Buttle had seen Rymer in the crowd.

PC Piper's report was also routine. He had written a lot about the Revellers jumping into the lead at Cross Street but the dull prose revealed he saw nothing odd in that. It happened every year. Piper had also seen Rymer in the crowd. The man must have been standing directly below me in a doorway otherwise I must have seen him.

I walked round the room with Piper's report in my hand. My colleagues' plain words made all my imaginings childish. At ground level the Revellers had appeared as silly and as harmless as they did every year. I sat down, reread my own report. It was just as dull as Piper's. I decided to see if he was in the station. I put on my jacket and walked to the door.

Sergeant Bone's clenched fist almost slammed between my eyes.

'Watch it!'

'Sorry, Jack. Just going to knock when you opened the door.'

'Uniformed branch taking it out on the Filth? I can see the headlines. I was just coming out to look at the duty book.'

'And I was just about to inform you that the Chief Constable wants you. That's why I knocked — nearly.'

'What's on?'

'Could be trouble, but looks the kind

you enjoy. You'd better get in there now.' Bone's eyes were sparkling. 'Can I check the book for you?'

'No. Thanks all the same. I wanted to know if Piper was on but that'll have to wait now. You not going to tell me any more, Sarge?'

'No need. You'll see what's up as soon as you do as you're told.'

'And up you too!' I said.

As I walked along the corridor I saw Cloag's head poke out of a doorway. Then an arm snaked out and made a furious beckoning gesture. 'Hurry up!' yelped Cloag.

I obligingly doubled my pace and halved my stride. Cloag was using me to impress someone with his powers of command. In the doorway I stepped up against Cloag and our jacket buttons clashed. For a moment we quickstepped nose to nose.

'Come in!' It was Slinfield who shouted. The dance routine with Cloag, and the sight of my red-faced Chief Constable pulling impatiently at the edge of the door, distracted me. I was

47

unprepared for the shock of the introduction.

'Detective Sergeant Green from London,' said Slinfield. 'DC Bull.'

'Good after — ' My voice died away as I stared at the seated figure. My hand was shaken and returned to me; a familiarity that further confused.

'Yes,' said Slinfield, with enormous smugness. 'A lady colleague suits the case, don't you think?'

Complacently, Detective Sergeant Green smoothed her short skirt. She was enjoying my confusion even more than the Chief Constable. But she was also shrewd enough to recognize anger.

'Er — ,' said I. 'How *do* you do, Sergeant. I suppose you're one of a team?'

'Cut that out!' snapped Cloag. 'No time to indulge your odd sense of humour.' Obviously *he* knew nothing of any other strangers. 'I want you to take our visitor on a tour of Clapton. Make sure she's got the feel of the place.' I tore my eyes away from loveliness and looked at Cloag. Had he really said that? He had.

'Yessir. I'll help her get the feel right away.'

I floated from the office, heard DS Green thanking the Chief Constable for his hospitality during the past week. I was even more confused. She'd been in Clapton a week and I'd not spotted her. And why need a guide after a week here? I heard her light step behind me, looked back at her towering, golden slimness. She would not be taller than me in bed. Later, I was to recognize that my flippancy covered something close to fear. In view of all the terrible events that followed it was odd that I should have been fearful then rather than later.

At the desk Bradninch was gulping like a stranded whale. Bone was dropping and picking up and dropping the same piece of paper.

'DS Green and I,' I rolled the words on my tongue, 'are going on a tour of Clapton together — both of us — with each other. As I still have my radio from last night I may even report progress from time to time.'

Bradninch made a peculiar hawking

noise deep in his throat. Bone put his piece of paper in a file, dropped the file. Green, probably used to having her leg pulled, was nevertheless delighted by her reception. She leaned forward and rested her magnificent bust on top of the desk.

'You could get arrested for those — er that,' said Bone.

'I'd come quietly with you. But perhaps one of you gallant gents will be kind enough to send my case up to the Royal. I've already booked in there but my case is still in Sir Bertrand's car.'

'Yesmaamsergeant,' moaned Bradninch, pushing Bone aside.

Then the fooling had to stop.

'Who's this?' snapped Green. She was so quick the door was still swinging as she spoke.

Turning, I saw the small, tired grey lady stepping hesitantly toward the desk. 'Why Miss Stigg,' I said, 'Is anything wrong?'

'I'm not sure. I don't know at all but — '

'Take your time, ma'am,' said Bone, stepping round the counter and gently grasping her arm. 'You know me and young Jack here and Sergeant Bradninch. And this lady is a colleague of ours.'

'Oh!' Miss Stigg was not made any happier by these introductions. 'Well it's — I may be making a fuss over nothing but my sister thought that perhaps we —'

'You tell me,' said Bone, 'then I can advise you.'

'Well, I — we think something's happened to — gone wrong — with one of my staff, one of my girls.'

'What d'you mean?' Bone was sharper than intended. But he knew, we all knew even before she replied.

'One of my girls has disappeared.'

With four giant rolling strides Bradninch was at the door of the radio room shouting at the duty controller. Pre-arranged signals began to rip over the town. Bone led Miss Stigg, now in tears, along the corridor to meet the unsuspecting Chief Constable. Green clamped onto my left arm with a paralyzing grip.

'Car?' she demanded.

'I walked in.'

'Damn! Mine's not here either. How far to the Stigg place?'

'Only three minutes walk. It's just round — '

'Show me! Come on, out!'

# 6

I was dragged out of the station. It was no use protesting about predetermined duties, hopeless trying to escape her grip. She was as strong as she was lovely. And at that moment I did not want to escape.

'Which way?' she demanded.

'Let go my arm,' I cried. 'You'll bloody break it!' I was released but subjected to a withering glare such as women do not usually give me. 'Follow me!' I ordered.

She clutched my hand and we began to run. I did not want to run but she insisted on running and I insisted on leading. Detective Constables do not usually hold hands in the street, or anywhere else, with female Detective Sergeants. As I was shunted along the High it was all too clear she was going to shake me up in more senses than one.

'Tell me about Stigg,' she demanded.

'Has guest house with sister Edith. She's Ethel.'

'The girl?'

'No ideas. They use three or four at a time every summer season.'

'Bent?'

'Hell, no! The Stiggs are clean, pure even. Expect their girls are too. They're very careful about staff — claim to run a genteel place.'

I was glad there were no more questions. The bloody woman was running me ragged. Skittering up the steps of the Avondale Guest House we came face to face with Miss Edith Stigg.

'Police,' I said, lifting the old lady back into the entrance hall. 'Ethel sent us. This is Detective Sergeant Green.'

'Oh — er — thank you for coming so soon but — '

'Girl's name and room?' snapped Green.

'Oh, it's — it's at the very top of the stairs, the door facing. Anna — Anna Duras. She's — '

'Don't fiddle with that radio now, Bull. Come on!'

Green grabbed my arm again but this time I wriggled free and raced for the stairs. I reached the fourth landing ahead of her, flung open the bedroom door and collapsed against it. Green sprang past to the dressing-table, snatched up a framed photograph. 'This must be the girl — and the photo's dated and signed last year. She won't've changed much. *Now* use that radio!'

Struggling for breath, I accepted the photograph. The girl stood between two nuns; all three had been staring blank-faced at the camera. I envied them their passivity. I switched on the radio.

'T-Tango Seven. Tango Seven calling Red One. Tango Seven calling Red One. Over.'

'Red One here. Receiving you, Tango Seven. Over.'

'Operations Room. Cloag!' I was beginning to enjoy myself again, was amused by Green's raised eyebrows.

'*Detective Inspector* Cloag here.'

'Bull, sir.'

'Where the hell are you? You've a job to do and — '

'Sorry, sir. I'm with Detective Sergeant Green as you ordered.' There was a muffled exclamation from Cloag. 'We're in Anna Duras's room. Description of missing person follows.'

'Hold it!' said Cloag.

I heard the click of a switch, knew that the next words spoken would be taped and also heard by everyone in the Operations Room. As I described the girl I could hear Green questioning Miss Stigg who had just arrived at the top of the stairs. Then Green was pressing herself against me, whispering more information. 'Bed not slept in. Girl last seen on way out to watch procession.'

I pushed my left leg hard between Green's thighs while transmitting this information. I lifted my knee very slightly. Green spoke again. 'Dinner served early so all staff could see procession.' She passed on this information while stamping on my right foot.

'Ho-Ho-Hotel served dinner early so guests and staff could see parade.' I tried to keep the anguish out of my voice.

Standing well apart we passed on

information that the girl was French, aged twenty, had been contacted through a reputable London agency, had worked for the Stiggs for about twelve weeks. No knowledge of any close relatives living in England. She had been in the country some time.

I stared at Green while I talked. She really was a peach, especially with that angry blush against gold hair. She looked a little uncomfortable as well as angry, pushed her hand inside her jacket to her right shoulder. I grinned, guessing at a broken shoulder strap from that mad gallop; not surprising in view of the figure to be supported. My grin conveyed my understanding. She became even angrier.

'Any photo?' asked Cloag, thinking I was transmitting a verbal from Miss Stigg.

'Yes, sir.'

'Get here with it — now! We'll run off prints. Meantime we'll send out the verbal. What's Green doing?'

'Interviewing the other Miss Stigg.'

'Tell Green to carry on. She want you back?'

'Yessir,' I said, without checking. 'I'm on my way, sir. Out.'

'Coming back are you?' asked Green, sharply.

'Cloag's orders. See you.'

Approaching the station, I was impressed by the stream of uniformed colleagues setting out to prearranged locations and tasks. Slinfield could organize. Within minutes of receiving the missing person report he would have twenty-five per cent of his men deployed and working, another twenty-five per cent on the way. In less than an hour every member of the Force would be engaged in the first stages of a massive search operation. No one would be spared unless he was too ill to leave his bed. The case carried absolute priority. Slinfield had put the matter quite bluntly at briefings before carnival week began. A fourth girl missing was as serious as a fatal assault on one of us.

The Operations Room was crowded. Slinfield was there, eagle eye on the first paperwork. Apparently, he had decided the situation was serious enough to leave all the rest of his county in the hands of his deputy and assistant. Dan Thirkettle, in old sweater and slacks, was writing notes; hands still dirty from the garden. Cloag was as immaculate and fussy as ever. No strangers were present.

'Photo?' said Cloag.

'Here, sir.'

'Get this to Hicks at once!' Cloag thrust it at a uniformed constable who scuttled from the room with it.

'The Super knows?' I asked.

'Of course,' said Cloag, huffily, resenting the implications of the question. 'He's driving back from Harmsworth now. You check this transcript of the description you gave. I want a quick word with Sir Bertrand.'

Despite all the activity, and there were nearly a dozen men in the room, most of them using telephones, there was no confusion. But there was something odd about the atmosphere, a feeling almost tangible and shared by us all. Ironically, it was a sense of relief. There were no more doubts. No hypothesis based on coincidences would now be convincing; not for *four* girls. And just for a short time, before public and political pressures developed, there were no fuzzy edges to the case, no conflicts. It was simply a manhunt. Someone had a fresh corpse to dispose of and that is a very difficult thing to do. No one was bothering with the possibility that Miss Duras might be in a strange bed sleeping off the effects of the carnival.

The door of the Operations Room banged open and Detective Chief Superintendent Shalvin lurched in. He was wearing a suit but his tie was under one ear and a shoe lace was flapping. Dozing on his bed or waiting for evening TV I guessed.

By the time Shalvin had been brought up to date by Slinfield and Cloag, a uniformed constable was standing in the doorway with a dripping print in his hand.

'Nice one,' said Shalvin, inspecting the photograph. 'Get that in circulation.' He turned to me. 'Understand you got that from the girl's room, Jack.'

'Yes, sir. DS Green is waiting there for me.'

'Oh, is she? You'd better get back then.'

'Right, sir.' As I left the room I wondered why Shalvin was looking shifty again.

I went to the car park, collected Green's case from the Chief Constable's driver and hurriedly departed. I meant to make the most of this new freedom. The real action might revolve round the girl from London; several kinds of action if I was lucky.

At the guest house I found the two Miss Stiggs reunited and dithering in the hall. They fell on me.

'Mr Bull, isn't it?'

'Yes, ladies.'

'We are — we are a little concerned about your lady colleague. She is a colleague isn't she?' Edith spoke while Ethel shook.

'Yes. I thought it wise to have a woman's view on this disappearance,' I said, straight-faced.

'But she wants to stay here — and in Anna's room,' said Edith.

'And it's a chambermaid's room,' gasped Ethel, made bold by the enormity of the suggestion. 'Not at all suitable for a guest.'

'Don't worry, ladies. She probably wants to be right on the scene of the — er — on the spot. You can see how this might help us.'

'Oh — will it? I see.' Edith bit her lip. 'We do look after our girls, you know, but we can't treat them *exactly* as if they were guests.'

'Never mind.' I decided to twist the knife a little. 'She'll want you to treat her exactly like Anna. Call her at the same time in the morning, offer her the same job here. No, I mean it, ladies. She wants to get the feel of how Miss Duras was — er — is living.'

I clumped up the stairs. By the time I reached the attic I was smiling. I knocked on the door, was invited in. DS Green, unaware of trouble just made for her, was sitting on the bed drinking tea.

'Thanks for the case,' she said. 'Drop it over there. I'll unpack later. I've had a quick look round — nothing. I'm waiting for your lab. boys to arrive. Fancy a cuppa, courtesy of the Stigg sisters?'

'Amongst other things!'

She paused in the act of pouring tea into the second cup, looked at me.

'Look,' she spoke very quietly. 'I know about your sense of humour. I know your nickname's 'Randy' and I know what it means. Why don't you stop acting up to your reputation?'

Irritated, I sat down, not on the chair but next to her on the bed. 'Why?' I asked. 'You got two sexy boyfriends down here with you already?'

'Perhaps you need a little help,' she said, smiling wickedly. She emptied the cup of tea, fortunately with milk added, directly into my lap.

I gave a shriek of agony, rushed out onto the landing, ripping down my saturated steaming trousers and pants. Standing there groaning and clutching at myself I could hear her laughing. Worse still, when I could at last see through my tears, I found myself confronted by the Stigg sisters, their horrified faces turned up toward me from the lower landing.

# 7

Monday, 07.15–08.00 Hrs

I sang in the shower for reassurance not joy. Life had conspired to injure me twice in the same place but I was still tenor. I looked again. I might go bald, and those red scald marks looked like something else. As for prowess — only time could heal and tell.

It had been a wretched wakeful night with just a sheet draped over me; my scalded parts throbbing with every movement. In each waking moment some embarrassing detail of the assault and its aftermath returned to mind. The poor Misses Stigg had never before seen and never would forget. Dragging soggy clothes back into my crotch, bellowing an explanation about an accident with hot tea had not prevented them scuttling away in panic. Determined not to seek refuge with my assailant, I had dripped down the stairs behind them until they turned into their room. As I'd slunk past their door the bolt had rattled home. That had been insulting enough but meeting the lab. boys on the next landing had been worse. Their ribaldry had pursued me to the street and, by this morning, it had reached the station and would be lying in wait. I was tempted to telephone and say I was still too sick to work but that would only delay and worsen my reception. I expected no mercy from colleagues who had worked through the night while I had rested with what the doctor described as a 'minor domestic accident'.

Dressing extremely slowly I thought about the dilemma facing me. The desire to work with Green had been considerably diminished. To continue as her assistant would really rub salt. I shuddered. On the other hand, staying with her might spare me a lot of agonizing leg work. Wishful thinking! DCs do not get that kind of freedom of choice. Green might not want me or Shalvin not release me. And there were those strangers on the scene, men to whom Shalvin had deferred. Perhaps the Chief Constable had already called in the full strength of the Yard. The pressures on him to do so were rapidly growing. If the local Force made no progress by the end of carnival week, which was Tuesday, only one full day away, the presence of one female sergeant would not check the shrill cries of the media.

The doorbell rang. Carefully zipping my fly I walked cowboy style across the room, down the stairs and opened the front door.

'And what do *you* want?'

'Ask me in, Jack,' said Green, smiling. 'I'm here to apologize. But answer the phone first.'

'It's not bloody ringing,' I snapped. The telephone rang. 'Hell! You'd better come in.' Confused by her clairvoyance I stepped aside.

'After you,' she said. 'Don't keep Shalvin waiting.'

Climbing the stairs was worse than descending. Bowlegged, unable to hurry, knowing she was following, I was further embarrassed by a muffled sound she uttered. I glared down at her. 'Didn't say anything,' she said, hastily.

I picked up the receiver, stood with legs apart.

'That you, Bull? Shalvin. Listen, boy. You're relieved of all duties here so you can work with DS Green.'

'Including the bank job, sir?'

'Including everything! I've persuaded the Chief Constable that Green can continue to operate without calling in any of her colleagues. You stay close because if she turns up anything I want you there as my eyes and ears. Make sure she has all the help she needs. Got that?'

'Yessir.'

'Good. With a bit of luck this could be a big thing for you. Stay with it. Keep me informed.'

'Sir.'

'Just arrived has she?'

'How did you — '

'Just agreed timing. Pull yourself together for Christ's sake! The ball's in your court.'

'Sir.'

'That reminds me. Just one more thing: a message from us all. Don't get your fingers burnt — as well!'

Replacing the receiver, I turned to face my new boss.

She eyed me warily. 'OK Jack?'

'It'll bloody have to be.'

'Good,' she said, with false heartiness. 'Not had breakfast? I'll get it for you while you finish dressing. Don't argue. Accept it as part of my apology. Then we can start again with a clean slate.'

Groaning and cursing, all the words I hadn't thrown at her, I struggled into shoes and socks. Then I stayed sitting on the edge of the bed and listened to her finding her way about my kitchen. I had not had a woman do that for some time. Her husky voice made romantic a simple query about my preference for eggs. I just grunted. She was too easily blunting my suspicions, quietening my hostility. Our relationship was developing against a bewildering background of half-understood complications; self-preservation demanded I stay suspicious. I walked quietly into the sitting-room. Her large shoulderbag was still in the armchair. I opened it.

The hair on the back of my neck stood up. A small pistol pointed at the bridge of my nose. Cautiously I checked the safety catch, started to breathe again. Her warrant card was straightforward enough, too straightforward to be lying under the butt of a pistol. But there was a second card: red, overprinted in black. It gave her powers beyond her rank. She could direct senior officers to render assistance without any reference back to her own bosses. In circumstances involving national security she could direct the work of any officer in any police force up to the rank of DI. In some remote corner of my mind other and more personal items were noted. Under her radio were purple briefs, lipstick, compact, purse. I closed the bag and left it in the chair. Rubbing my hands over my face I walked slowly into the kitchen.

'What a super place you've got!' She stood in front of the cooker, wearing Jeannie's apron over her summer print frock and looking sixteen. There was a pain in my throat. I blew my nose hard. I supposed it was the loss of Jeannie, having this woman in my home, over-work, many things, all things. She put her hand on my arm. 'Jeannie's apron?'

'Doesn't matter.'

'I'm very sorry about her.'

'We'd been engaged a month. Then some hit-and-run bastard caught her.'

'But not caught himself?'

'Right. Seems likely she was hit by a small black car. Not many small black cars about. We never got a whisper — not a repair job, respray or dumping.'

Silent moments. 'Angels passing,' said Green, nervously.

'Maybe. You like my home, then?'

'Yes — and the view.'

'We can eat out on the roof if you like.'

She hesitated, then chose to eat in the kitchen. I began organizing furniture and, forgetting my disability, did myself harm moving a chair.

'You all right?' she asked. I bit my lip, nodded. 'I really am sorry about that but you did ask for it.'

'Balls!'

'Appropriate,' she sneered. Then we both laughed.

'Come off it, Sue.'

'What did you call me?'

'Sorry — er — Sergeant.'

'That's not what I meant and you know it. How did you know my name? You checked my bag already?'

'So?'

'Team point for initiative. Now you sit down. Eat and listen. You need telling — in several respects.'

'Aren't you eating?'

'No, you bugger! Miss Ethel Stigg had me up at six for breakfast. Said it was your idea getting me into the girl's routine. It's bad enough being in the poor kid's lumpy bed, never mind the six a.m. start. And I told your Miss Stigg where to stick *her* apron. She didn't need much of your encouragement to think of me as a heaven-sent replacement. But that isn't telling you why I came here is it?'

'No,' I said, truculently.

'Quite simple. The idea was to get a woman into the town before carnival week started, to give her a full briefing and see if she could turn up anything all you men had missed. The arrangement also had the advantage that if someone vanished this year both County and Yard could show they had co-operated even before the tragedy. That's one reason why a local WPC wouldn't do. The other was that local villains don't know me.'

'So you've been here some time?'

'Since last Monday, two days before carnival week began.'

'But that's a week today. Where've you been hiding?'

'Not hiding exactly — just being discreet. I stayed with the Chief Constable and Lady Slinfield. I've been wandering around — saw you several times. I'm pretty good at staying in the background.'

'You bloody must be! But why hide yourself from me? You sure you're telling me the whole story?'

'More coffee please,' she said, smoothly. 'And while you're pouring think about the important questions, the ones an intelligent copper like you might ask after searching my handbag.'

'Sergeant, are you wearing knickers?'

'Jack, you're a fool.'

I leaned across the table, kissed her hard on the mouth. Then, holding her round chin between my hands, I stared into her lovely, lying cheating face: the glowing skin, grey eyes, straight nose and that ripe, red mouth. She made me feel sick.

'You *are* a glutton for punishment,' she said, softly, making no attempt to free herself. 'And you've just poured me this hot coffee.'

'Sue, I reckon we don't really need each other.' I released her, sat back in the chair.

'Look,' she said, taking off her blonde hair.

'Oh, no! No!' I nearly vomited. 'How the hell — Put your wig back on for Christ's sake!'

'Sorry, Jack, but if you want to join the grown-ups you have to know the score.' She replaced the wig, but I could still see, would always see, that bristle-covered scalp with its terrible wound. 'It's OK. I'm better now and once my hair grows — ' She was trembling slightly.

'Tell me, Sue.'

'Right,' she was falsely brisk. 'And it's Susie, by the way. You know that different branches of our intelligence services can no longer work independently of each other or of the police. The lone agent's a rare bird these days. My job was, still is, to liaise between my department and the Yard. I had a foot in both camps. My rank is my proper rank, if you see what I mean.'

'That fits with the cards you carry and which you meant me to find — sooner or later. But it don't fit with Clapton-on-Sea. There's something else going on. You're not going to tell me all these missing girls are, were agents?'

'No. I'm here simply as a Detective Sergeant and also for the good of my health. On my last job my cover was blown — hence the state of my head. It would have been fatal if the men backing me had been much slower.'

'But who would do — ?' I stopped, disgusted by my own naïvety as much as by concern.

'I was betrayed on an anti-terrorist operation,' she said. 'After I was rescued I was finished on that job. That, and being ill, meant I had to pull out of active service for a while. The doctors advised rest but not complete inactivity. My boss came up with the bright idea of a change of scene plus a straight job as police-woman. So I was loaned to the Yard and here I am: safe and almost completely sound.'

'Sorry about the pass.'

'Look, Jack, I know you've been screwing your way round the town for the last two months, like a kind of therapy, but any kind of pass helps a bald girl's ego no end.' She laughed. I didn't.

It was not my mistrust or resentment that kept me silent but the knowledge of what was under her wig. Someone, another human being, people, had taken a noose of thick wire and put it round her head just above her ears and about three inches above her eyes. Then they had tightened or perhaps burnt it into her skull. Whatever the doctors had been able to do, and I had seen the wound in its healed state, they had not been able to fill in the deep purple crack that passed round her head like a blistered parody of the crown of thorns.

# 8

'Shall we take my car?' I asked, hand on the garage door.

'From what I've heard it'll be too conspicuous. But I know you're dying to show off.' I raised the door and she clapped her hands. 'It *is* true. You do have an old Rolls.'

'And why not?'

'A symbol of your independence, your bloody-mindedness?'

'Several've said that, darling. At one time it was even supposed to be evidence I was bent. Though who in Clapton'd bribe a young DC on this scale I can't imagine. But no one loves a copper with money of his own. It means the Force can't buy him either. Where's your car?'

'Round the corner, outside The Drum. Mine's only a Mini.'

'Better take that then.'

'Time?'

'Eight-fifteen. Hell! As early as that?'

'Your fault, clever clogs. You arranged for me to be called at six, didn't you?'

'So I did. But it's already hot enough for mid-morning. It'll be another scorcher today.'

The Drum public house, smelling of warm, stale beer, faced blankly onto the hot deserted quay. The fishermen were long gone. A solitary cat stretched on the bench by the saloon door, uncurling itself to a sun that would soon send it stalking shade.

I stood between the pub wall and the red Mini waiting for Green to unlock the car. As I looked toward her I saw, just behind her left shoulder, the alleyway down which I had chased that unknown watcher. Perhaps I had been chasing her.

'What's wrong?' She was smiling at me.

'Nothing much. Just gotta go back up to the flat for a moment. Hang on.'

Despite the pain in my crotch I went back into the flat and laid out some black cotton threads as a check on intruders. When I had finished with these precautions I looked out of the small rear window facing away from the sea and onto the street. I could see the Mini. Green was sitting inside and using her hand radio. I walked down the stairs both slowly and thoughtfully.

Back at the car I lowered myself gently into the front passenger seat.

'Penny for them?' she said.

'Just awaiting orders, Susie, Sergeant. And listening to the engine you've switched on. This is no ordinary Mini. Now command me, lovely lady.' Suspicion made me stilted. No acting honours for me.

'Two things. Give me a route that leads to a really quiet private spot where we can talk. Second, as I drive through town, tell me something about the place, something I can check my own impressions against.'

'Go straight along the Front. First right past the end of The Hill. What do I talk about first?'

'No. You decide. How you begin is important to me.'

The car moved forward forcing a cooling breeze through the open windows. For a few moments I watched her driving: immaculate, of course. I relaxed. There were things to say for which I never had an audience. Mistrust of her need not prevent me talking about the town.

'Sexy place, Clapton. Full of body consciousness or something. Hard to say why. Partly holiday trade — for some reason we appeal to the sex-mad young. They come here to copulate like birds in Spring. My theory is that it's the site, stuck down here between two hills, very sultry, makes glands overactive or something. Clapton is sort of Clochemerlian if you like.'

'Blimey!'

'Yes, Miss. Difficult to put into words but real enough despite absence of data! Something about this case seems to fit the setting. But you have to guard your imagination pretty carefully here. And your tongue! Imagine how some of my colleagues would react if they heard this kind of talk.

'But don't get me wrong. I'm not damning the place. I've certainly enjoyed the sexy side of life here! But it's very pleasant in other ways. All the things you'd expect from WI to a small art gallery. Community-minded place, good facilities for the old, etc. Not bad for thirty thousand population. Doesn't offer opportunities of Bristol or Southampton, say. But only the young leave for the better jobs elsewhere. They all come rushing back at summer weekends to lay the visitors.'

'And you?'

'Lay the visitors or leave? Before Jeannie was killed I never wanted to do either. Now I'm not so sure. As for the job — well. One problem is lack of promotion, not just because we're a small force but also because we've a particularly bloody chief constable — been almost unhinged over these girls. No promotions in Clapton while this case is unsolved.'

'Tell me about the missing girls.' She glanced at me again instead of watching the road. I was beginning to feel like a snake working on a partially hypnotized but still resisting rabbit.

'The girls in order,' I said.

'First to go: Olga Pozniak, West German of Polish parents. *Au pair* to

Colonel and Mrs Tremayne. Not clear why she was needed; they have plenty of staff and no children. Olga vanished night of procession three years ago. She'd been in Clapton ten months. Dark hair, blue eyes, poor complexion, stringy figure. Five feet-six inches. Age nineteen. Dad came over: very aggressive until size of problem explained to him. No dad likes idea daughter might want to vanish. That only happens to other fathers — the bad ones. Lawyers keep contact but we've turned up nothing.

'Second: Helen Fazakis, Cypriot, *au pair* with the Wilsons. He's local headmaster. They've got five kids. He reported girl missing the day after the procession two years ago. She was twenty-two years old then. Black hair, dark eyes, dark complexion. Plump and five-feet-two. Reported working as garage attendant in Exeter. False lead. Some family queries by letter and via the London Embassy, that's all. Apparently gave up when we failed, or else decided as she was twenty-two it didn't matter. Amazing how often relatives of missing persons don't seem to care very much. Probably why they go missing! The Wilsons were the people really distressed. She'd been with them since the previous Christmas having met them in Cyprus the summer before that.

'Third: Pat Marsden, British from Londonderry. Domestic help, skivvy rather, for our Chief and Lady Slinfield. Worked almost a year. Blonde with grey eyes. About five-feet-seven. Rather fat with well developed figure. Only nineteen years old. She vanished on carnival night last year. Hell, that sent the balloon up! Tell you more about that later. We had letters from an orphanage where she was brought up, also several visits from a local Catholic priest. And that was another one: gone. You know about number four, Susie.'

'Pretend I don't.'

'Anna Duras. French. Unattractive, dark-haired girl, no tits. About five-feet-six, age twenty. Worked as chambermaid for Stigg sisters. Came from same London agency as Olga Pozniak. No links with the other two girls. One answered local paper advert, the other was the holiday acquaintance. We're working on Anna Duras now.'

'Let me check, Jack. Except for their vulnerability no connection between all four girls: not between homes, not between recruitment. None of them ever met?'

'Not to our knowledge.'

'Any link between employers?'

'Only one — very heavy respectability. We've found nothing there. They don't even link up socially. Wilson and the Chief Constable have never even met. They move in quite different circles.'

'But you now believe the disappearances are linked?'

I hesitated for a moment.

'You can imagine how much we've discussed these cases. For perfectly good reasons, timing, etc., the earlier disappearances were thought to be linked. Now this new one will certainly be tied in with the others.'

'You think that's wrong?'

'No, not wrong. Everything points to that conclusion. Four disappearances at the same time of the year, same place, girls with similar jobs, no intimate friends, all single and away from home. Everything points to the same cause, perhaps to same person or persons unknown. Very convincing.'

'Why the doubt?'

'Not doubt, exactly. More a feeling we ought to be investigating the *less* likely possibilities.'

'What do you mean?'

'Not sure. But there are some odd things. It's very hard to dispose of a body — never mind four! And one man disposing of four bodies is quite likely to choose the same spot. Four graves make quite a disturbed area. If buried separately he'd soon run out of really good hiding places. And they'd have to be bloody good. We've torn the town and the county apart in the last three years; even checked the meat stocks in all the cold stores! It's also unlikely the bodies are in the sea. Very difficult to dispose of bodies permanently in the sea.'

'So?'

'It raises some less likely ideas, don't it?

How about white slaving for a start? Don't bloody snigger! It's not completely impossible and it would explain why we can't find any bodies. That sort of idea suggests odd things about motive as well. Perhaps the deaths and or disappearances are linked as properly organized kidnappings. That's very nasty because the motive can't be financial — the girls had no money and there've been no ransom notes. I suspect that motive is particularly nasty sexual.'

'You could be right. Shalvin tells me you've a nose for trouble.'

'Does he? Turn off along that track. So you've been talking to my senior officer?'

'I've talked to *all* your senior officers and he's the only one who likes you. You've marked your card with most people.'

'Too true. Firstly, I'm public school educated and have money. Secondly, they've little time for intuitive thinking, imagination, whatever you like to call it. Every answer has to be found in a file nowdays.'

'And you've no time for paperwork?'

'Not true. Not a case of either — or. We need both together. In the long run, routine can only get routine results in routine cases. And we certainly haven't got a routine case right now. Yet, while you and I sit up here on the moor, my poor bloody colleagues are sweating their way through house to house, memo to memo, file to file, for the fourth time in three years. And what will it do? Dishearten, exasperate, lead nowhere. Worse still, it hardens attitudes, strengthens prejudices. It's that much harder to admit you might be on the wrong track after a whole County Force has been worn out looking for leads through routine checks. Stubborn sods!'

'Calm down, Jack, and don't exaggerate! It's only since Slinfield's girl vanished that you've been much involved. Before that they were just names for Missing Persons.'

'What this case looks like from the outside and what it feels like to be stuck in it are two very different things!'

'OK! Point taken. Tell me where we're going on this track.'

'We've arrived. This is Hangman's Moor. Very appropriate. Down in that dip over there is a very pleasant pub we can visit when the sun is high.'

'A very wide open moor,' she said, nervously.

'That's why it's so private,' I said, spitefully.

We lay on her car rug; she on her face, me on my back — I had no choice. After a few minutes she raised herself on her elbow.

'I'm damned if I'm wasting all this sun. D'you mind if I sunbathe?' She sprang up and stripped off her flowered dress. She was no longer stocky but all legs, thighs and high bust. Looking up, I saw her body, cupped and clasped in purple bra and tiny purple pants, standing golden against the hard blue sky. I felt myself rising, could not stifle a groan. Her laughter ran clear across the moor. 'Sorry, Jack. You don't have much luck with me, do you?'

'Not so far,' I whimpered. This was the third time I'd suffered pains in the same place since the carnival procession. This association of facts made me laugh as well.

She knelt beside me, those incredible breasts inches from my mouth. Very gently, I put both hands under them, did not hold, just lifted very slightly. They barely moved. The long hot summer moment passed while we looked at each other.

'Something special, you and I, Susie?' I heard the words, knew their meaning, knew the significance of the moment. But within me the more cautious, suspicious or experienced part of myself was using very different words. Why was she so free, so charming? And why was she acting, so successfully, the role of fantasy dream girl? She was just a fraction too good to be true. Even her underwear was a little too well chosen. And for God's sake, what was she doing sunbathing up here when she was posted to investigate a major crime? Distracted by the inner voice, I was momentarily confused by her answer to my question.

'Perhaps so, Jack, perhaps.' She drew back, her breasts easing from my hands.

'But this is no time to get yourself even more heated. Besides I must take my hair off. The doctors recommend the sun.' The naturalness of her response conflicted with my suspicions, made me clumsy.

'Must you, Susie?'

'You can always keep your eyes shut,' she said, icily.

'I'm sorry. I didn't mean — '

'Forget it.'

Dismayed by my foolishness and her response, I was even more alarmed to discover that the freakishness of her appearance still further excited me. It was disgusting.

'I'm sorry to damage your susceptibilities,' she said, angrily.

'Liar,' I said. 'You damaged 'em yesterday and you're making things worse today. You're not sorry.'

'Well, let's have a quiet kip on it. Good for the temper. Then you can tell me the story of your life.'

# 9

## Monday, 11.00–12.00 Hrs

'I was an abandoned baby. Stop laughing! The vicar found me in the porch of Stedwell Church out near Harmsworth. He and his wife adopted me. Being relatively old they both died in my late teens and within six weeks of each other. He couldn't live without her. Being reorphaned, as it were, was one reason for joining the Force. It gave me independence earlier than if I'd gone on to college. The Rev. left me a little money and I thought that was all. I never suspected he'd also left me a small fortune for when I was twenty-one. His lawyer was sworn not to tell me because the Rev. feared that the knowledge might damage me.'

'That hurt?'

'Not when I thought about it. After all, he knew nothing of my parents. They

91

were never traced. My dear mother had already demonstrated her irresponsibility. And bad blood will out, especially if you know all that money is waiting for you — plus the Rolls you saw in the garage.'

'So you don't need to be in the Filth?'

'Christ! They didn't leave me that much. Anyway, I'd started my career before I knew about the money. Most of it went into my very nice flat and garage.'

'But you mean to stay in the Force?'

'If I get a fair deal. If not, sod 'em all bar one.'

'Pushy Jack Bull, eh?'

'You wouldn't dare talk like that, lying next to me half-naked, if I wasn't incapacitated.'

'I knew what I was doing yesterday, didn't I?'

'Don't spoil it all, Susie, not now you've sweetened me by letting me talk about myself. How about telling me your story?' I said, mockingly.

But there was no story. Instead, she drew a quick breath, grasped my arm. 'What's that noise?' she demanded.

Alarmed by the nervousness in her

voice I sat up and looked into her face. 'It's only a helicopter, I think.'

She grabbed her dress, began to wrench it over her head and shoulders. I was just going to make a joke about excessive modesty when her face burst clear of the dress.

'Susie, what's the matter? It's on our side, you know; lent us by the army. We work with them when a search is on.'

'I must get to the car,' she said, woodenly. Her eyes were black holes in her skull. Her fingers fluttered wildly at the belt of her dress.

'You don't like being too long in open spaces, do you? That's why you didn't want breakfast on the roof. If I'd realized it was this serious — '

'Well, now you know. Shut up and help me, you bastard!'

I held her close, ran my hand through the stubble of her hair, avoiding the scar. The helicopter traced a line above the edge of the moor, dipped out of sight into the valley. And all the time she was shaking in my arms. The summer silence crept back onto the moor. The empty idiot sky beamed on us. Susie watched me pick up my jacket and the car rug.

'All right now?' I asked.

She nodded, wiped away the blood from her bitten lip, clumsily shrugged into her wig. 'Thanks,' she said, unsteadily. 'That's the first time I haven't run for cover.'

The car was a firebox. The steering wheel burnt my hands. 'Wherever you're taking me — let's move,' she muttered. 'Get some air in the car.'

'We're early for the pub but we could sit in the garden — under the trees.'

'Yes, please. Go!'

We did not speak again until we were sitting in the pub garden under the great oaks. The cool shade was as soothing as fresh linen against sunburn. Slowly, we revived, and by the time the bar opened we were hysterical with laughter at the stories we had shared. But in her laughter I could still hear the faint echo of a panic-stricken cry.

A subtle change in our relationship had come from that moment of fear. The revelation of her weakness had given me a weapon. Whatever her intentions, her undisclosed plans for me, if the in-fighting got dirty I had a means to hit back. I would swear that she was unbalanced.

'Don't remember when I've laughed so much,' she said, when I returned to the lawn with two foaming tankards. 'Suppose we'd better get back to business now.' There was a slightly apologetic tone in her voice. She was slipping. My reply was correspondingly more firm.

'Not 'til I've downed my pint and got refills.' There was a short silence.

'That didn't take either of us very long,' she said. 'My treat. I'll fetch them.'

'No. You pay, I'll fetch. Just getting back into my stride.' I could hear her giggling as I waddled across the lawn.

'Business now,' she said, firmly, when I returned. 'Tell me, how did all the employers react to the disappearance of their girls?'

'With genuine concern. No reason to suspect any of them being implicated. Colonel and Mrs Tremayne were stiff upper lip about it but also genuinely upset. Mrs Wilson made the biggest public scene — cried a lot at the station.

Her girl being the second to disappear she immediately assumed the worst. Yet, in an odd way, Sir Bertie's distress was the most marked. He was almost irrational about the case. But you stayed with him for a week. You must've formed impressions of your own.'

'Some. But you carry on.'

'But where are we going with this line? You're not suggesting one or all of these employers are responsible? Not Mrs Wilson, the Misses Stigg or, dammit, our Chief Constable?'

'I suppose not. But, let's face it, we're prepared to consider *any* possibility aren't we? And what a marvellous cover — being Chief Constable!'

'Jesus! You're not safe to be let out.'

'Bet you quite fancy the idea, really.'

'The Chief Constable! That'd be a — well — '

'Save your breath, Jack. You won't live to finish that beer! Let's try another line. See if you bite. Concentrate on Anna Duras for a moment. What worries you most about her disappearance?'

'Everything,' I said. 'Including the fact

you and I are sitting here taking a holiday on the case and talking rubbish at the same time.'

'Calm down. It's my responsibility — remember? If you're so worried think of yourself as another of my interviewees. Answer my question!'

I remained silent, drank the last of my beer. Reluctantly, I acknowledged there was nothing to lose by co-operating — at least, not yet.

'I'll tell you what worries me most,' I said. 'In the face of all the publicity about security, the obvious way our men were lurking everywhere, etc., the bastard calmly went ahead and abducted another girl. No, let me finish. I'm not *so* worried about the fact it's a terrible slap in the face for us. What really bugs me is that the person or persons involved must be mad, reckless mad in a way I can't begin to define because I don't understand it. And how do we catch people like that?'

She stood up. 'The answer may come to you while I'm driving us back into town.'

And that, I thought, is where co-operation bloody well gets me.

# 10

Green stopped the car on top of West Hill. Below us the town, promenade, beach and sea glared up against the noon sun. People swarmed like ants through the streets, hauled themselves across the promenade and fell stupefied onto the beach.

'God, it's hot!' she said, scratching under her wig.

'Just think of the poor buggers on house to house. That'll make you feel better.' I knew how it felt to be there: early afternoon, almost too tired to reach down for the latch of the silly wrought-iron gate of Mon Repos; heat reflecting from the white concrete path; trying to concentrate, pretending this particular housewife might be the one to give the vital clue, yet knowing she is going to be as woolly, unhelpful and confusing as all the rest; leaving her still yapping on the doorstep; looking along the road at the endless waiting ranks of sun-blasted houses; not leaping the fences (as if one could!) but politely moving up and down the parallel paths of The Larches, Sea View, Bide A'wee, Restmore; regretfully refusing offers of hospitality; knowing that as soon as one's fist closes on the glass Bully Bradninch will come tiptoeing past. With every house checked the conviction grows that nothing will come from the exercise, not even the titillation of the bored housewife opening her dressing-gown while talking. It is always someone else who finds that sort. One cannot even linger to flush out the shirt-tailed adulterers skulking at the stairhead praying the woman can get rid of the unexpected caller. I sighed for my colleagues.

'Penny?' said Green.

'Not worth it.' But she seemed to have guessed my thoughts anyway.

'They're obsessed aren't they?' she complained. 'Obsessed with finding the body rather than the motive. What are the reasons for killing? Why repeat it? How is it done?' There was a long silence. I had decided her questions were not meant for me. She was not pleased. 'I suppose all we can do is re-interview the bereaved employers.'

'Oh, no!' I groaned, self-pityingly.

'Well, it's all you've got to offer, isn't it? Otherwise we're reduced to sticking pins in the electoral roll.'

'Can't offer what we haven't got. Perhaps there's something for us at the station.' She took the hint and started the car. 'If we are going back over old ground maybe we should call on the Tremaynes first.'

'Because their girl was the first to go?'

'Er — yes. There might be another reason. Colonel Tremayne is on the board of a construction company. I've always thought a building site was a good place to hide a body permanently.'

'We all think that,' she said, impatiently. 'But they were all checked anyway.'

'Not until the third girl vanished. Until then we'd stayed with routine enquiries. No reason to do otherwise. When that third girl vanished we checked back over all the sites every builder had built on in the last three years.'

'Better late than never.'

I did not reply. She knew as well as anyone that hind-sight makes fools out of every police force. I could have told her that every current building site had been sealed since yesterday, that not a brick could be laid or a cubic foot of concrete poured without us knowing about it. But if she had decided Clapton was Hicksville why should I waste my breath persuading her otherwise.

As she drove the Mini slowly along the seafront I had reason to break the silence. 'Stop here!' I said.

'You sick?' she asked, parking the car. I was, but that was not the reason for stopping.

'No. See that man limping along — there — outside the amusement arcade?'

'Blond, thin man, narrow-faced? What about him?'

'Pete Rymer, Carver Rymer.'

'I know *that*. Seen his mug shots.'

101

'Oh — er — well. How about him for our villain?'

'Reason?'

'Only an idea. Better than pins in the electoral roll. He's got some very odd friends, believe me.'

'You got it in for him?'

'Not exactly. He's known of course. Four years for GBH. Slashed a tart's face with his razor.'

'Come off it, Bull! Too right he's known. We also know why he limps don't we? You broke his leg!'

'I tried to arrest him and he pulled his razor.'

'But that's not his story, is it? According to his brief you broke his leg *after* you got the cuffs on him.'

'Is that likely? And me in my first year of service at the time.'

'Hmm.' She looked directly at me. 'Very likely I'd say. Especially if you were wanting to teach him a lesson, make your mark. And the judge made some rather pointed interventions during your cross-examination.'

'What you *think* might have been a

judge's private opinion is no sort of *proof.*'

'Never mind, Jack, I'm not. Just avoid the trap of believing that rat Rymer is now harmless.' She restarted the car.

'I'm watching him,' I said, feebly.

'So am I,' she said, still sharp. 'Saw him carnival night, in Quay Street, just around the corner from Cross Street.'

So, she'd been in Quay Street had she? But that wasn't the important thing in what she had said. Something almost surfaced in my mind. No good pressing it — better wait, think round it. That information needed storing for some reason that went deeper than the fact yet another person had seen Pete Rymer when I hadn't. We completed the journey in silence.

At the station there was a new problem. News of the disappearance of Anna Duras had leaked out and the place was under siege by Press and TV.

'It'll have to be the back door,' said Green, irritably.

'Straighten your wig,' I said, spitefully. 'You might appear on telly and be recognized by your old terrorist friends.'

She jammed on the brakes, swung the car at the car park entrance and pounded the horn. The gentlemen of the Press scuttled out of the way.

'Temper!' said I.

We beat the Press by a stride. Dan Thirkettle slammed the door behind us and locked it against the mob.

'Thanks, Dan,' I said. 'What you doing here?'

'Might ask you the same — and you, Miss.'

'Oh — this is Detective Sergeant Green from the Yard. DS Thirkettle, local CID.'

'I know,' she said. 'Hello.'

'Er — hello. I've just been watching TV recordings of part of the carnival parade,' he said, reverting to my question.

'Any help?' I asked.

'No,' he said, miserably. He looked absolutely wretched. I supposed him to be disappointed as well as tired. 'Whaddya want?' he asked.

'Shalvin,' said Green, curtly.

'Good luck to you,' said Dan. 'He's in the CID room and he's got the Chief

Constable with him. Sir Bertie's in the helluva state. Wants someone's blood — maybe yours, laddie. Just something to offer the Press.'

'What's the trouble?' asked Green. Again I got the feeling Dan didn't want to speak to her.

'Well,' he said, reluctantly, 'We've just looked through every bit of TV film of the carnival procession and found out they've only got coverage of the start and finish. Nothing on the rest of the route, so no hope of spotting any funny business. I think Sir Bertie hoped to see our kidnapper in action. When he complained to Shalvin in front of me and Cloag, Shalvin reminded him he had himself ordered that cameras could not film at positions where our men had been placed. To be made a fool of in front of us really got him mad. Worse, we both confirmed what Shalvin said. Not that creepy Cloag was very happy about doing that!'

'So — Sir Bertie's upset,' said Green. 'Let's get in there while he's still jumpy. Leave the talking to me, Jack.'

'I'll say,' said I, raising my eyebrows at Dan. He did not respond.

In the CID room the atmosphere crackled. Sir Bertrand Slinfield, red of face, was sitting at the desk, Chief Superintendent Shalvin, angry, and Inspector Cloag, worried, were standing stiffly against the wall. Green and I stepped into the room. Dan shut the door behind us. In the moment of silence that followed we could hear his foot-steps echoing away down the corridor and, very faintly, the brayings of the newsmen in the street. Cloag coughed nervously.

We all looked at Sir Bertie. His colour faded slightly but the atmosphere was no less tense. In some other indefinable way the atmosphere did change and we were all aware of it. We had brought a new kind of tension into the room and it *had* to be something about Green. *I* didn't know what the hell was going on. Shalvin was alert, anticipatory, unlike Cloag who resented our arrival.

'Well, Green,' said Shalvin, quietly. 'Do you and Bull wish to report to me? The Chief Constable is as interested as I am.'

Green stared steadily at Shalvin.

'Er — Inspector Cloag,' said Shalvin, 'would you please see that all the film next door is safely repacked and returned to the TV reps? They're sitting in our canteen waiting. Make the right noises on our behalf, will you? No need to tell them the films were NBG.'

Cloag looked angrily at the Chief Constable who inspected the desk top. No help there. Cloag stamped out of the room, slammed the door behind him. The tension tightened another notch.

'Well?' said Shalvin.

'No report yet, sir,' said Green. 'But we want your agreement to proceed on a definite line.'

'Yes?' said Shalvin, eagerly. The Chief Constable stood up and pretended to look at a wall map.

'We'd like to re-interview *all* the couples who lost their *au pair* girls before the Stiggs lost Anna.'

'That can be arranged,' said Shalvin.

'Dammit!' shouted the Chief Constable. 'You've no right or reason — what I mean is, why should Lady Slinfield and

I have to go through all that again?'

'With respect, sir,' said Shalvin. 'How can you be left out? What would other people make of that?'

'Well I — ' The Chief Constable got no further.'

'Be quiet!' said Green. An awesome silence filled the CID room. I wondered if I should kneel. 'Sorry, sir,' said Green, unrepentantly. 'But you know I can demand the Yard be called in at full strength. I came alone because the arrangement suited you but if I don't get full co-operation I'm going to start shouting for help. A fourth girl has just vanished, I say how I want to proceed, and all you can do is argue the toss about the type of co-operation I can expect.

'Don't you shout at me, young woman!' shouted the Chief Constable.

'You have our full support, Green,' said Shalvin, quickly. If you can tell us anything of a lead we'll be glad to hear it. If you can't I'll give you until Wednesday morning. After all, *you* would also like to make some progress before we call in the Yard.'

'Thank you, sir. We understand each other,' said Green, smiling. One liar to another, I thought.

'But surely — surely we are entitled to expect some information,' spluttered the Chief Constable. 'If she's so keen to cross-question us again then for all we know she thinks one of us made off with the wretched girls.'

'Is that so unreasonable, sir?' she asked. He was at last struck dumb.

'Tell me, Sergeant,' said Shalvin, with a quick, nervous glance at Sir Bertie. 'Are you saying you have a lead on these disappearances?'

'Not directly. I'm afraid your searches have to continue.'

'Are you suggesting these four cases are not all connected?'

'No. I'm sure they are.'

'You go along with this, Bull?'

'No — I mean yes, sir.' I was alarmed at being dragged into the firing line. My hesitancy revitalized Sir Bertie.

'D'you still need him?' he demanded, pointing at me.

'Yes, sir. Invaluable man,' said Green, straight-faced.

'One of our up and coming,' said Shalvin, solemnly. Green bit her lip.

Sir Bertie gave a shout of baffled rage and stomped to the door. Hastily, I opened it for him. 'Come and see me at twelve noon, tomorrow,' he snarled.

'Yessir,' I said, closing the door.

'Siddown you two,' said Shalvin, falling into the chair behind the desk. 'Christ! What a bloody shambles! You'd better deliver something in the next few hours, my girl.'

'We'll try,' said Green.

'You do realize our carnival week runs Wednesday to Tuesday to catch two weeks of holidaymakers? So if you're following a line involving current visitors you've only got one more full day after today.'

'Yes, sir. But this is a local job or jobs. Everything points to it.'

'You go for murder, then?'

'Nothing else fits. Four disappearances at the same time of year, four successive years — that's not compatible with ordinary cases of disappearance. I'd

110

believe one girl might read of a case in the newspapers and decide to ape it the next year, but another two after her. The other thing is that with all the fuss repeated each year one of the girls must've heard about our enquiries and come forward — if she could.'

'And it's all local?'

'Yes, sir.'

'You're very positive. So why haven't we found a body or bodies? You know how hard it is to hide a corpse.'

'You haven't found them because you've always looked in the wrong places. That's not meant to be cheeky nor can I suggest the right place. But that's the feel of this business to me, sir.'

'Another nose here, Bull?'

'Could be, sir.'

'You take the point though?' asked Green.

'Of course I do,' said Shalvin, wearily. 'All the possibilities point to local crime. And I believe in noses. Trouble is, after so many years searching, thinking and speculating, what one believes seems unreal, unlikely. The fantastic becomes attractive.'

'True enough,' she said, standing up. 'It's the fantastic we're dealing with. We must push on now, sir.'

'Anything you need?' asked Shalvin, wistfully.

'Only to continue with a free hand,' said Green, gently.

'Anything I can do?' Shalvin was trying very hard.

'Two related things, sir. Firstly, let's step up the pressure even more. Someone must have seen something odd in at least one of these cases and either hasn't realized it or is protecting someone. Since your men are all chasing Anna Duras they can easily revive the other cases at the same time.'

'And the second thing?'

'Arrange for us to interview Colonel and Mrs Tremayne this afternoon. This may be a good time to reopen old wounds.'

# 11

## Monday, 14.00–14.30 Hrs

### TRANSCRIPT OF INTERVIEW WITH COLONEL AND MRS TREMAYNE

*Annotations by DC Bull*

*Acting on instructions from Detective Sergeant Green I secretly recorded the interview by means of a tape recorder hidden in a large holdall. The holdall also contained two radios issued by DS Green and this was to be our explanation if questions were asked. As cover I also took notes of parts of the interview.*

*Green (G):* If you're ready at last I'll knock.

*Bull (B):* Knock away, Susie — er, Sergeant.

*Colonel Tremayne (T):* Good afternoon. You must be the policemen — er — man and woman we're expecting. Your colleague — Shalvin isn't it? — he telephoned me earlier.

G: That's right, sir. I'm Detective Sergeant Green — my card. This is Detective Constable Bull.

T: His card's in the bag, no doubt.

B: No, sir. I keep our radios in there in case we're called. I'll get my card out if —

T: Don't bother. Seen you about, young feller. Suppose you'd better come in. My wife.

Mrs Tremayne (MT): Good afternoon. I hope there's no sort of trouble. We —

T: I suggest we wait until we're all in the drawing-room before we start gossiping.

MT: Oh — yes. Er — this way please.

T: Will you sit there with the lady next to you?

G: If you don't mind, sir, I would like this seat by the window.

T: Well, please yourself. I'll stand.

G: Yes, sir.

T: I must say I'm puzzled by your visit. Your man was not at all helpful on the telephone. I told him my wife and I know nothing of these ladies who keep a hotel. We certainly don't know their staff.

G: Quite, sir. But we are enquiring about the disappearance of Olga Pozniak.

MT: Oh, no. Poor girl.

T: But that was years ago. She hasn't been found?

B: Would that surprise you, sir?

T: What do you mean by that remark?

B: Exactly what I said, sir. *Pause.*

T: It's all so long ago. What is it — three years?

G: Almost to the day, sir.

MT: I suppose we would be surprised after all this time, dear.

T: I've no idea. I'm more surprised the whole wretched business is being raked up again.

B: I'm sure you wouldn't say that if it helped us to trace your girl.

T: You people have had long enough to find her.

B: It's not just a question of time, sir. It depends very much on public co-operation.

T: You've had enough of that from me. All those interviews, embarrassing enquiries into my private affairs. I haven't forgotten any of that, I can assure you.

Hardly my fault she chose to run away.

G: You believe that, do you, sir?

T: What?

G: She ran away.

T: Er — yes. Why not? Flighty young things, you know. Some of them.

G: I don't know, sir. Are you saying your young lady was flighty?

MT: A very nice quiet —

T: I'll answer the question if you don't mind.

MT: Yes, dear.

T: I have no idea if the young woman was flighty. She was here to help my wife and other staff with the entertaining. We do a lot of entertaining, you know. I think it fair to say I play a significant part in local affairs.

G: That could make you vulnerable, sir.

T: I don't see the point of that remark. Your attitude —

G: The point is someone may have been tempted to make capital out of her disappearance. Has that happened at all?

T: I find that suggestion offensive. None of my friends were other than sympathetic about our troubles over the girl.

B: And your enemies, sir?

T: Don't be impertinent. I think you had better leave.

B: We'll wait in the hall while you say goodbye to Mrs Tremayne.

T: What the devil do you mean?

G: You don't seem to appreciate the seriousness of our enquiries, sir. We are co-operating with you by coming here. If you order us to leave we will do so but our enquiries will have to continue at Clapton police station.

T: This is outrageous! I'll telephone your commanding officer at once.

G: That will be an assistant commissioner at New Scotland Yard.

T: Oh, will it? Then I'll ring your local man.

B: That's good, sir. You'll get my chief. If I could have a brief word after you I can ask him to issue the warrant for your arrest. Actually, he's the chap who phoned you earlier.

MT: Please, George!

T: But, dammit! You're suggesting —

G: We're making no suggestions at all, sir. We're interested simply in how other people acted and have acted toward you as the former employer of a girl who vanished. *Pause.*

T: Very well. I suppose there was a certain amount of silly humour behind my back.

G: What form did this take, sir?

T: Well — there were attempts at suggestive remarks.

B: Masculine humour, sir?

T: Yes, very much so. But no more than that. I certainly made sure that sort of thing was suppressed. And it's not something I wish to discuss any further in front of my wife.

MT: That's all right, dear.

T: No, it's not. I suggest you ask another question.

G: Yes, sir. Was the disappearance of the girl ever referred to in any other ways that you found offensive?

T: Only by the police raising the whole business all over again.

G: I didn't mean that, sir.

T: Then what did you mean?

G: Has anyone attempted, in any way whatsoever, to connect you with the other girls who disappeared? *Pause.*

T: You know what I think of all your questions.

G: Do you wish me to repeat my last question?

T: No. And of course the answer is no.

B: Not even through masculine humour, sir?

T: Don't be a fool, young man. Of course there was some — er — leg pulling.

B: Nothing more?

T: I see no point in this at all. You're just victimizing us because our *au pair* ran away three years ago and you look silly because you can't find her.

B: That's not the cause of our concern, believe me.

G: Is that really what happened, sir? She ran away?

T: Yes, of course it is. She just left. Probably didn't like working in a properly disciplined household. These young girls get very sloppy if you don't watch 'em. My wife's too kind-hearted sometimes.

G: Olga left her possessions behind.

T: Yes. But not much to leave behind, if you ask me.

G: If things happened the way you say, sir, you would not expect to be blackmailed in any way.

T: Certainly not!

MT: Oh!

G: Yes, ma'am?

MT: Nothing. Nothing. It's just that you make the world seem a very wicked place.

T: That's not news. All right. I accept your line of argument. But the answer is still no. No pressures, no threats, no blackmails, whatever you like to call 'em. No one as successful as I have been can be damaged by silly gossip.

G: I'm sorry to say it has gone beyond a matter of gossip.

T: Gone beyond?

G: DC Bull and I are now investigating the kidnapping and murder of four girls.

*Long pause. Colonel Tremayne was either shocked or frightened.*

T: You — you don't — . Are you suggesting there is a connection between our girl running away and the disappearance of any other girl? That two girls —

G: Four girls, sir. Not two. One every year, at the same time, in the same circumstances.

*Long pause.*

T: But why did you say murder? You haven't found any bodies. How can you say you're investigating murders?

B: Excuse me, sir. Who said we haven't found any bodies?

T: But you can't — I mean it would all be in the Press.

B: Not if we don't tell them.

T: You're mad, both of you. There's no connection between Olga and these other girls. I'm positive. You're wrong, quite wrong.

G: You're very sure about that, sir.

*Long pause. Colonel Tremayne sat down next to his wife.*

T: You must understand. I — we — we feel responsible in a way. Olga was — . Well, she was the first to disappear. I don't want people pretending that in some way I set off all these horrible events. You've got the wrong idea, I'm sure. Clapton isn't the place to look at all.

G: Do you have some other place in mind, sir?

T: What? Oh — well — no.

B: Sorry, sir. This is undoubtedly a local crime. Vile it may be but someone here is responsible; perhaps several people — a group of some kind.

MT: But that means we may know them — actually —

T: Shut up! *Pause.* I'm sorry. What my wife is trying to say is — is people as prominent as us know so many people. What you are suggesting is disgusting.

G: I quite agree with you, sir. We are both sympathetic to your point of view. Unfortunately, in murder cases in this country, the very large majority of the victims knew their murderers — often lived under the same roof in fact, were —

T: Christ!

MT: Oh, dear.

G: Are you all right, sir?

MT: My husband has an ulcer and —

T: Be quiet, woman! Where did you put the new tablets?

MT: In your bedroom, dear, on the bedside —

T: Right. Excuse me for a few minutes, slight inconvenience.

MT: I'll come —

T: No. You stay here. Answer their damnfool questions. You've nothing to worry about. (*Spoken with some emphasis.*)

*Colonel Tremayne left us to go upstairs.*

G: While we're waiting we can ask you a few questions about your girl, Olga Pozniak.

MT: I don't really want —

G: The colonel said you could do so, ma'am.

MT: Oh — well —

G: Did you like Miss Pozniak?

MT: I beg your pardon?

G: Did you like her?

MT: I suppose so. Yes. It's not something one thinks about when hiring staff.

G: Did she like you?

MT: Your question seems rather —

G: Did she? *Pause*. Did she?

MT: I presume so. She was a very quiet girl.

B: Did she work well?

MT: Not always. But you know what

young girls are. Not that I was severe with her — nor was Maud.

B: Maud?

MT: My housekeeper.

B: Of course. She did not resent Miss Pozniak being here?

MT: Certainly not. Why should she? She was glad of the help.

B: Even when the girl made mistakes?

MT: Er — yes.

B: Did you ever warn Miss Pozniak she would have to go if her work did not improve?

MT: No.

G: Did Colonel Tremayne like Miss Pozniak?

MT: I never discussed the matter with him.

G: Why not?

MT: Running the house is my business and George leaves me in charge. I know my duties.

G: Duties, ma'am?

MT: I endeavour to be a good wife.

G: But Miss Pozniak could not have lived under the same roof as your husband for all that time without him ever expressing an opinion.

MT: You must ask him when he returns.

B: We will be doing so, ma'am. He was legally Miss Pozniak's employer, wasn't he?

MT: I suppose so. *Pause*. He once told her she was spotty and ate the wrong foods.

G: Really? Did your husband often make personal remarks of that sort?

MT: Not in my hearing. I don't understand what any of this —

G: Who gave her permission to go to see the carnival procession?

MT: What? Oh, I really can't remember every trivial detail after all this time.

G: Whoever gave her permission might, in a sense, be responsible for her disappearance.

MT: How dare you! I refuse to answer any further questions. You have upset my husband and now me.

G: I must advise you to reconsider what you have just said. We must look ahead in a case like this.

B: In case my report is referred to by other officers during their enquiries.

Better for all if I don't have to write down your previous answer.

MT: Oh, dear. *Pause*. Well, you see, it wasn't a question of permission, not really. My husband — *Pause* — er — he offered a lift into town.

*Pause*.

G: Why was this never mentioned before?

MT: My husband thought it would be misinterpreted.

*Long pause*.

B: If she had been in any sort of trouble who could she have spoken to?

MT: To me of course. But there was never any need.

G: We must doubt that now. Who spoke to her about her work being bad?

MT: I never said it was bad. If there was any minor problem Maud usually dealt with it.

G: Usually?

MT: Well, perhaps my husband might also have mentioned a matter if he thought it necessary.

G: But you just said that running the house was your business, part of your duties.

MT: Well — yes, generally. My husband is so busy.

G: Did the colonel like her?

MT: I've already said —

G: He was fond of her?

MT: Really I don't —

G: Took a fatherly interest, ma'am?

MT: You could say that, I suppose.

G: You thought the colonel was getting too fond of her?

MT: What do you mean by —

G: You were worried he might miss her a lot when her year with you was over?

MT: I suppose — I never really thought of it in those terms.

G: How did you think of it?

MT: I don't quite —

G: We know young girls so easily forget their place these days. Was she flattered by your husband's interest in her?

MT: Well, she would be, wouldn't she?

G: I beg your pardon, ma'am.

MT: Oh. You know: his rank, money, business success.

G: And being an attractive older man?

MT: Er — yes. Not that there was anything —

G: Anything what?

MT: Well — improper. You keep interrupting me. *Pause.* The colonel is a gentleman.

G: But poor little Olga Pozniak was no lady.

MT: I resent the implications in that remark. I am quite sure that even if she had — had not behaved properly my husband would have done so. I suggest you refer your rude remarks to him.

G: Yes, ma'am. Would it be possible to speak to Maud now?

MT: She's not here.

G: Your other staff?

MT: They are all out — afternoon off. Except Henry — the gardener.

G: Do they usually have the same afternoon off?

MT: Not usually. My husband suggested that as you would be coming and it was such a lovely day —

B: So he took that decision about running the house. Strange for so busy a man.

MT: Please. He's not at all well. He's got a bad ulcer.

They may have to operate soon if —

128

*Mrs Tremayne began to cry.*

B: I'm sorry to hear that. How long has the colonel been ill, ma'am?

MT: About two, no, nearer three years.

B: About three years.

MT: I think I should go and see how he is. Please —

G: There he is in the back garden. If you will excuse me, ma'am. I'll go and talk to him out there. Can't have him unnecessarily upset.

MT: No. Oh, all right. Thank you. I'll make some tea.

G: Thank you very much. I'll leave DC Bull here with you. Perhaps you could arrange for him to interview your gardener?

MT: Yes — er — yes. I'll just go and tidy up.

*Mrs Tremayne left the room wiping her eyes.*

B: Bingo!

G: You thinking what I'm thinking?

B: He took her into town that day. We can check back on his original interview statement. See if he's got any kind of alibi.

G: I don't know. We're certainly on to something. But what?

B: Trouble is it need not relate to our case at all. Perhaps we're just intruding into a rocky marriage: a lusty, nasty old man and she can't cope.

G: Seems pretty brittle — the marriage. And a reference to separate bedrooms.

B: You think Olga was a bedmate?

G: Possible. Also interesting he couldn't do the arithmetic about the number of girls disappearing.

B: And ill for the last three years. Begins to fit almost too well, perhaps?

G: Makes you wonder.

B: Go talk to the man, duckie.

G: And you! Give me about ten minutes before you fetch us for tea.

B: Is that how long you can defend your honour?

G: Your impertinence is being recorded.
*DS Green went out into the garden. I went into the kitchen taking the holdall with me.*

MT: Oh, it's you.

B: I thought it more friendly to come out and join you.

MT: I'll just put the kettle on, then I'll take you to see Henry Thomson. He's working on the rose border beside the front drive.

B: Sorry to be so much trouble, ma'am.

MT: That's not important. I'm more concerned about George. He's not been at all well these last few months. I expect he's had some business worries.

B: I'm sure he's worried about Olga as well.

MT: Yes — of course. But you young people forget that three years is a long time in the life of a busy business executive.

B: Not if we're policemen we don't.
*Pause.*

MT: Would you like tea in about fifteen minutes? I will allow you that time with Henry. He's down the drive just beyond the big rhododendrons. I'll ring the bell for you when the tea is ready.

B: Thank you, ma'am. I know my way. We drove in by that entrance.
*Pause. Walk down the drive.*

*Henry Thomson* (H): Aar, Bully boy. I saw you comin' in.

Some woman with yer. Trust you!

B: Colleague.

H: So you say, bully boy, so you say. But if you be truthful you won't mind what I jest seen.

B: What?

H: She's gorn out ter the quarry with the colonel. Saw 'em through the bushes. Came round the side the house they did. Walkin' close they were.

B: All right, Henry, you old lecher. Keep your imagination under control while we have a chat. I want to check with you — . What was that?

H: Sounded like a gun. Where you orf to then? What about this 'ere bag?

Bleedin' coppers. Only speaks ter yer when them well wants . Right stuck up bastard 'e is. 'Im and that other'n Cloag. Right pair. Let's see what's in 'is bag then. Aar. Er — .

*Thomson may have realized the bag contained a recorder. Nothing was touched.*

# 12

I pushed the tape transcript away from me. Also on the desk was a copy of my carefully worded report of what happened next. No need to read it; recollection was perfect.

I had hurdled those rose bushes in one huge stride, my cry of anguish almost drowning Thomson's shout. As I raced across the open lawns toward the old quarry the sun hurt me almost as much as my scalds. If I'd dared to delay I would have ripped off my jacket. The contents of the pockets pounded against my sweating body. I crashed into a shrubbery and emerged onto a small grassy plateau beside the quarry.

She stood alone. As I halted twenty feet from her she raised her right arm in an odd half-defensive gesture. The expression on her face silenced me. She pointed down into the quarry. I walked to the edge.

Colonel Tremayne lay face down at the bottom of the thirty-foot cliff, a mark darker than shadow at his head. I did not even consider the possibility the man was still alive. I rounded on Green. Her face had smoothed out, was expressionless.

'This how you re-open old wounds?' As I spoke I remembered what it was that weighed heavy in one of my pockets. I drew out the pistol and pointed it at her. She made a soft hissing sound, seemed to shrink and hunch like a tautened spring. I stepped toward her then, warned by the gleam in her eyes, stopped.

'Sergeant,' I said, as calmly as I could, 'throw your bag on the ground.' She looked at me thoughtfully. I had the shocking impression she was not considering my gun at all. I tightened my grip, holding the gun two-handed. She shrugged the shoulder strap off her left shoulder, carefully placed the bag at her feet.

'Step away from it! Back to the edge of the quarry. Further!'

'Easy, Jack,' she said, raising her

eyebrows. 'I'm likely to fall.'

'Just you bloody well concentrate on that possibility!' I knelt by her bag, opened it, took out her pistol. It had not been fired. I had some difficulty looking at her.

'Silly sod,' she said, amused. 'If you'd asked I'd've told you. He used his own gun. Went over the edge with him.'

'Had to be sure.' I gave her the bag. As she took it I realized that the parallel tracks we had been following had somehow merged. Her purpose for being in Clapton had something to do with myself not with the case we were working on. My purpose, to find the missing girls, had merely been a scenario for her investigation of me. But now the case united us. Together we had made some progress if only to a death.

'You must've been thinking some very odd things about me since we met.' She was as aware as I that we were in the moment of change.

'Yes,' I said. 'But not too odd. I've just returned your gun — loaded.'

'Thanks very much! And now I'm

wondering about you. Didn't know you'd been issued a pistol.' Her tone was slightly querulous.

'I haven't,' I said, pausing to enjoy the Kafkaesque moment. 'It's a toy. Picked it up carnival night.' She uttered a very coarse remark — twice.

'You been down to him yet?' She shook her head, glumly. 'Then I'll go.'

Colonel Tremayne lay face down in his own blood. The gun was trapped under his body. I slumped down on a large boulder and looked at the corpse so slowly stiffening under the hot sun. What had the man known or feared? What had we trespassed upon? And what would happen to *us* having let this awful thing happen? My thoughts were cut by laughter from Green as she sat next to me on the boulder.

'No one ever dared take me with a toy gun before. Something new every day.'

'This new enough for you?' I snarled, jerking my head at the corpse.

'Sorry,' she said. 'Suppose we'd best send for the wagon.'

'Yeah. And you can break the news to

his missus. That'll take the silly smirk off your face. What the hell did you say or do to the poor devil?'

'I asked him about his relations with the girl, and he said, very emphatically, that they were perfectly proper. But don't start pretending this is my fault. You're just as responsible. He must've picked up his pistol when he walked out on us. I thought he was a long time looking for tablets.'

'All right. Let's not waste energy blaming each other. But what else was said?'

'I asked him if it was true he had commented on the girl's appearance to her face and in front of Mrs Tremayne. Said he couldn't remember such a trivial thing. Then he said we shouldn't take too much notice of his wife. Said she's a very bitter woman and they weren't really compatible.'

'Sexually, did he mean?'

'I tried to make that point — tactfully, believe it or not — and he brushed it aside by saying they were incompatible in most ways.'

'You two got chummy pretty quick. Then what?'

'He asked how a woman like me had got involved in the case.

'I said something about it seeming a good idea because the case was all about women. Then he repeated my last words: 'all about women'.'

'And?'

'He drew his gun and shot himself in the face.'

'While you looked on in maidenly astonishment?'

'If that's how you want to describe it. Now use a radio and get that wagon.'

'Damn! They're both in that bag and I left it in the drive.'

'Then get moving, Constable. The speed with which you got here suggests you're feeling better — so run! I'll look after the body.'

'Bit late to be looking after him, Sarge,' I said, nastily.

I climbed out of the quarry and walked slowly across the lawn; my attention divided between the pain in my crotch and recollection of Tremayne's shattered face. I found the bag where I had left it. There was no sign of Thomson. As I took out a radio a final touch of horror stained the afternoon.

Tremulously, a bell was rung. I looked along the drive toward the house and saw Mrs Tremayne standing on the steps ringing a handbell. Her thin body was tilted slightly forward above her stick-like legs. She peered short-sightedly through her spiky-framed spectacles wondering why neither her husband nor the strange visitors answered the summons to tea. Her shoulders drooped, emphasizing the slight hump in her back. Then, hearing me speak into the radio, she straightened, smiled vaguely in my direction and resumed ringing her small brass bell.

I jerked upright in my chair. Exhaustion and recollection had almost caught me out. It would be another nail in if Cloag caught me dozing. The thought was apparently communicated to the man. I heard Cloag call my name from the CID room.

I walked down the corridor, stepped into the room, half-hoping Green would be there. I had last seen her in the Operations Room with Shalvin, had left her there when I came out to check my report. No sign of her now. I shut the door, turned to face Cloag who was sitting on the far side of the paper-strewn desk. Why were his shirts always so white? And the bugger never seemed to perspire either.

'Take off your jacket and sit down,' said Cloag, surprisingly.

I did both things and wondered what he was going to hit me with first. I did not have to wait long to find out.

'Right,' he said, fingering his despicable little moustache. 'Let's review the situation together. Ready?'

'Yes, sir.'

'Copies of your tape transcript, typed version of your report, bank statements for Colonel Tremayne for the last five years summarized by Detective Sergeant Thirkettle.' Cloag slapped each set of papers with the palm of his hand as he named them. 'Let's take them in that order. Agreed?'

I could only nod. For Cloag to be so

brisk, cheerful even, meant only trouble for myself.

'The tape transcript reveals that you allowed a witness to walk out of a police interview, obtain a gun and subsequently to shoot himself to death with it. What do you have to say?'

'That's not entirely a fair interpretation of — '

'Stop there, Bull. I'm not interested in talk about interpretations nor in attempts to place blame elsewhere — on that woman, Green. *I'm* not allowed to know what she's up to so I'm not interested in *her* complicity. My concern is getting you out of CID and back on the beat — always assuming they'll have you. Clear?'

I nodded. I was shattered, not by the degree of hostility directed at me (I had half-expected that) but by the bitterness in the man's voice when he referred to Green. But then Cloag was so intensely jealous of his own role and importance he must have been in mental agony ever since he discovered she reported only to Shalvin and the Chief Constable. Yes, I thought, she even had you sent from the room. I looked directly at Cloag. The man was actually licking his lips.

'But before you leave us, Bull, you can help clear up the mess you've created. You are probably under the impression that Colonel Tremayne was guilty of some misdemeanour in connection with the disappearance of Olga Pozniak?'

'Yes, sir.'

'But not necessarily that he murdered her?'

'Not necessarily, sir.'

'But thanks to your bungling we can't be sure.'

'No, sir.'

'Worse still, we cannot now seek to establish any connection with the other three more recent disappearances.'

'Well — er — not through Tremayne.'

'Bright lad! Hardly through Tremayne.'

If he expected any come-back from me he was disappointed. There was no point in arguing with a man so obviously convinced he was on top.

'Now for your report on events immediately after you stopped recording.

This is a copy of your written report additional to the tape transcript?'

I looked at my doctored version of what had been said at the quarry. I was surprised to see Green's signature at the bottom of the last page.

'Oh, yes,' said Cloag, softly. 'Madam agrees with you but is too busy to give me more than a signature. But it is your report?'

'Yes, sir.'

'Anything to add?'

'No, sir.'

'No changes you would like to make, other conversation to report?' Cloag was good enough to smell a rat but not good enough to catch it.

'No — sir.' I was not talking to *him* about toy pistols.

'Let's turn to the bank statements. By the way, allowing Tremayne to shoot himself at mid-afternoon was co-operative of you. The bank staff were still on the premises. Thirkettle has made a brief preliminary examination of the figures. Guess what he found?'

'No idea, sir.' No future in guessing games.

'Evidence suggesting blackmail.'

I resisted the temptation to share Cloag's delight. News that we might have been on the right track made Tremayne's death an even more serious blow.

'Read Thirkettle's comments!' Cloag tilted back his chair, pointed his hands for prayer and stared at the ceiling.

I picked up the paper. Dan had identified a change in Tremayne's financial habits commencing the month after Olga Pozniak had disappeared. Before that time Tremayne had run his personal account in the style of a rich man rarely using cash. But after Olga's disappearance he had begun drawing a lot more cash cheques. Dan had spotted a pattern. For a year the small extra cheques totalled about one hundred pounds per month. Then the amounts had increased giving a monthly total of two hundred pounds. That figure had remained constant ever since. Dan had presented a succinct conclusion: possibly blackmail at £100 per month, raised to £200 per month after one year.

Interesting that Dan had gone straight

for blackmail. Could have been a hundred other things: effect of inflation, discovering he liked cash in hand, secret gambling, women. But maybe Dan was right. Funny how blackmailers always think in terms of round figures. It's one of their sillier mistakes. But if it was blackmail the villain was cool; not too greedy, not pushing a rich man too far. The ante had only been raised once. Someone had been guaranteeing themselves a steady little income for life. Now the life had ended.

'Well?' said Cloag, impatiently.

'It could be blackmail, sir. Could be keeping another woman.'

'To replace the *au pair*?'

'That's a possibility, sir. But why did she become twice as expensive after exactly a year?'

'Interesting possibilities. But what do you suggest we do next, Bull?'

'We've gotta dig deeper on Tremayne, maybe through Mrs Tremayne, sir.'

'But that will take a lot of time and we're supposed to be calling in the Yard very soon.'

'They can help out.' I knew it was a silly thing to say, especially to a man so jealous of his own advancement, but I was sick of the cat and mouse treatment.

'But they can't help you out, can they, Bull?'

'I — '

'Tremayne got that pistol and shot himself while two officers were with him. What are the odds the Yard'll try and lay all the blame on the local lad — you?'

'I'm sure the Super'll back me up.'

'I'm sure he won't. Why do you think he's not here running this interview? He's done a Pontius on you. And who can blame him? We've been struggling for some kind of lead for three years and as soon as we get one you turn it into a dead end!'

'But that's not necessarily — '

'Shut up! You're out of time.' He took a deep breath. 'However, the problem of what to do with you is temporarily shelved — very temporarily! I have been instructed to leave you with your girl friend until she's finished with you as well. Then we'll have another meeting.

Meanwhile, remember I'm watching you very closely.'

'Thank you very much, sir. I'm sure you're not the only one!'

'Don't waste breath being impertinent. Just go away and — ' But I had gone, cutting off the final words by slamming the door.

I walked quickly through the station, ignored Sergeant Bone at the desk, pushed through the swing doors. On the steps outside I paused, surprised by the evening and the silence. A cool breeze from the sea drifted along the street, and the pressmen had all gone away. I walked slowly down the steps, along the street and round the corner. She was waiting for me of course.

'Hello,' she said.

'Susie,' I said, wearily.

'You look done in. Let me take you home. My car's round the corner.'

'Thanks.'

'How was Cloag?'

'Vindictive — as expected.'

'We wondered how you were getting on.'

'We?'

'Shalvin and myself.'

'Two rats abandoning the sinking ship?'

'Rubbish! We knew you could handle it. You're a big boy now.'

'Thanks!'

'Did the interview add anything to your ideas about the case?'

'Not really. Dan's ideas about the bank statements are reasonable. Could be blackmail.'

'Suppose so. Dan's pretty keen on that idea isn't he?' I said nothing. That wasn't her question. 'Is he offering a conditioned response from a tired police mind or is he covering for the lack of information? Too many people blackmailed into silence?'

'Ask Dan!'

'I'm asking you. I'm asking why the pipeline has failed and who's blocking it?'

'You're not suggesting Dan is?' For a moment I almost lost control of my anger. Then I regonized the similarity between her words and those I had spoken to Dan on carnival night. I was too shaken to fight the point.

'Here we are,' I said, stopping beside

her car. She walked round to the driver's door, looked at me across the car roof.

'Keep to the point, shall we?' she said, calmly. 'No ideas from Cloag at all?'

'Maybe a couple,' I said, grudgingly. 'Two questions he didn't ask. First, he missed the one about Tremayne's faulty arithmetic. Remember? Two girls not four? Why was Tremayne so shattered by the idea that all *four* disappearances were linked? Why was he willing to accept links between his girl and one other but not his girl and three others? Could it be that he was only blackmailed over the first two of the girls?'

'Possible. That might explain why the blackmailer only increased his demands once — when girl number two vanished. What was the other thing Cloag didn't ask?'

'It isn't always the killer who gets the blackmail notes is it?'

'Maybe not.' She unlocked the driver's door but did not get in. She looked at me again. 'Who's cool enough to blackmail a very rich man for only fifty pounds a week and keep it at that?'

I must have been irritated by her lack of response to my own question and the off-hand way in which she pitched her question into the fight. Curtly, I told her I knew several people in Clapton like that. When she pressed me for a name I asserted myself by saying we could check out the most likely suspect tomorrow.

# 13

Tomorrow had come soon enough. Too tired to sleep, I looked out onto the night-silver sea. I leaned on the window-ledge with both arms, steadying myself as the familiar room and view floated round me in shadows of blue and grey. Beyond my own breathing I could hear softer night sounds: the faint fluttering of mice in the loft, a sound that had always brought a chuckle from Jeannie. Outside, another sound: distant murmur of an engine. The moonlit sea was furrowed by a fishing boat, razor-sharp bow opening silver flesh, water knitting together in a frothing, glittering wake. It was a reminder of that scar round Green's head. I realized I was banging my fists on the windowledge.

Earlier, some of my anger had exploded in curt refusal to invite her into for the evening. Any expectations she had of soothing or testing my injuries, or of sharing my bed, had been crushed as brutally as I could manage. Her lack of resentment, her cool amused smile, had infuriated me still further.

Irritably, I turned away from the window, walked toward the great empty bed. As I slid under the sheet I felt as if Green was there embracing me in the white cloth, shroudlike, snaring me. But there was no time to transmute imagination into dreams. The telephone drilled a hole in my head. I snatched at my watch, 02.10, tottered into the sitting-room, picked up the phone.

'Jack Bull.'

'Detective Inspector Cloag here, Bull.'

'Sir.'

'There'll be a car at your door in two minutes. Come immediately to the station basement.' He slammed the phone down. The sound seemed to merge with the soft purr of the patrol car. I have no recollection of dressing or getting to my front door.

'What's up?' I asked Piper, as I fell

across the back seat. He set the car rolling before answering.

'Not sure, Jack. Looks big. They're moving things fast and quiet.'

'They're moving me too bloody fast. When am I getting a night's sleep?'

'You're doing better than most, Jack — you and your minor domestic accident. Think of all the legwork you've missed.'

'Stuff it!' I said firmly, and closed my eyes. But the adrenalin was flowing fast. If I was going to the basement then sleep was the last thing I wanted.

'It's you and me, Jack,' said Sergeant Bone as I stepped through the swing doors. 'Come on!'

We walked quickly to the stairs past uniformed and plain-clothes colleagues making their way to the car pound. No one was talking.

In the harshly lit basement, Bone and I formally identified ourselves. We signed for pistols and twelve rounds each. As I loaded six my hands were steady; not so my mind. The heavy weight, feel of the butt, shiny cartridges, faint smell of oiled metal, affected me as they always did. All that crap about arming our police not being risky. Of course we draw weapons to use them!

'What's on, Sergeant?'

'Someone's taken a pot shot at PC Buttle.'

'Missed him?'

'So I hear. We'll get details upstairs. Ready?' said Bone, calmly. He and the armourer were looking at me intently.

'Yes, Sergeant.' Hastily, I grabbed my spare cartridges.

'Let's go,' said Bone. As we left the armoury PCs Jenkins and Aplin came in. Soberly, we nodded to each other.

DI Cloag was waiting at the top of the stairs.

'We'll go together with Piper. Jenkins and Aplin can follow on,' he said. 'I'll tell you what we know on the way.'

We piled into the car. 'Junction Basset Street and Marine Avenue. Fast but dead quiet!'

'Sir,' said Piper.

'This is the situation,' said Cloag, looking back at us from the front seat.

'PC Buttle was going home about twenty-five minutes ago when he saw an old Bedford van being turned round on that small building site in Basset Street. Naturally, he was suspicious and, knowing we're keeping a special watch on building sites, he moved across the street. That was when someone took a shot at him. He took cover and radioed for help. By a stroke of luck there was a patrol car in the vicinity. It arrived too late to stop or chase the van but they've radioed back that they've trapped a man on the building site. The patrol car is parked in the back entrance. Buttle's watching the front.'

'And you want us to go in, sir?' asked Bone.

'If I think it necessary,' said Cloag.

We stopped at the end of Basset Street. The road was completely blocked by patrol cars, all with lights off. Sergeant Bradninch waddled forward.

'Both ends of Basset Street are sealed, sir. So is the back way out of the site.'

'Good. Any signs of life?'

'No, sir.'

'Where's PC Buttle?'

'He's still along the street keeping watch, sir.'

'Get him up here, quietly.'

Silently, we waited, fidgeting in the warm summer night. From the direction of the sea weak moonlight partially illuminated the town. But all the street lights were out, automatically switched off at 01.00 hours.

'Morning, sir,' said Buttle, hoarsely. The front of his uniform was covered in pale dust and his left cheek was bruised, presumably the result of diving for cover. We showed the deference due to a man of action but as he answered our questions he was obviously more aggrieved than flattered.

'Twenty-seven years in the Force with no trouble. And now some sod takes a shot at me — sir.'

'He's still in there?'

'Someone is, sir. And there's no way out the back. Our patrol car drove round the block just in time. They radioed they saw a man in the archway as they drove up. He turned tail and ran back inside.

He was carrying a shotgun or rifle.'

'Alone?' I asked.

'Dunno about that,' said Buttle, slowly. Bone looked at me.

'Did you get the number of the van?' asked Cloag.

'No chance, sir. As soon as the driver spotted me he put his headlights on and drove out the front gate. Then I heard a shot and dropped.'

'Looks like you frightened the van driver and he left a mate behind,' said Cloag.

'That's my figurin' as well, sir.'

'Now, Buttle, think carefully before you answer this one,' said Cloag. 'Did the shot come from the van or from the site?'

'Positive, sir — the site. Saw the flash.'

'You've had a lucky escape, I think. And you've done a good job.'

'Thank you, sir,' said Buttle, surprised. Praise from Cloag!

'Right. Let's get him out from there,' said Cloag.

'Him, sir?' asked Bone.

'No reason to believe there's more than one,' said Cloag, angrily. I sympathized with him. While he was risking his career Bone and I were fussing about risking our lives. I looked at Bone, saw his shoulders lift and drop. I swore to myself. We could have suggested waiting for Shalvin but Cloag obviously meant to seize 'his chance'. Hard luck Bone and I were the ones armed.

Ten minutes later the two of us were crouching to one side of the open gate of the building site. It was at one end of the high wire mesh fence fronting onto Basset Street. At the other end of the fence an unlit patrol car had been swung onto the kerb with lights facing into the wire. At a given radio signal the driver, who was lying on the floor of the car, switched on the undipped headlights.

The gunman fired at the car, blasting in the wind-screen but missing the lights. Bone and I rushed through the gateway and crouched in the shadow of a large concrete mixer. The driver flashed the headlights several times then switched them off. Deafened by the shot, confused by the leaping shadows thrown up by the car lights, Bone and I waited for our night vision. While we waited we had time to think about the gunman who was so willing to shoot. He must be involved in something desperate. But what?

We had entered a black box. On three sides moonlight was excluded from the site by high walls. To left and right the sides of the adjoining buildings were supported by huge timber frames. Facing us, the back wall shut off the street parallel to Basset Street except in the centre where it was pierced by an old archway. It was there that the patrol car had first trapped the gunman. We knew that the crew had now been joined by colleagues including Aplin and Jenkins, both armed. Their instructions were to keep off the site and only to cover the archway exit. Armed police approaching from both sides in darkness could lead to disaster. As my night vision improved I could see the patrol car blocking the narrow exit and facing toward me. I hoped the crew understood their orders. If they switched their lights on at the wrong time we would be blinded not the gunman.

I was pretty sure the last gunshot had come from the back right-hand corner of the site but our orders were quite specific. We were not to move forward until the next stage of the operation. I wondered how Bone was feeling. Then he tapped me on the shoulder. I looked at him and he placed the fingers and thumb of his right hand against my cheek. Five seconds. We both lay flat and closed our eyes. The car lights were flashed on again but we did not see it happen. It was the gunman's night vision we wanted destroyed. Then Cloag used the loudhailer, his words echoing flatly between the brick walls bounding the site. We opened our eyes, raised our pistols.

'You have no way of escape. All exits are covered. Come out with your hands up!'

No response. We waited. When Cloag began to repeat the same message Bone dived along the side wall and behind a great baulk of timber. I went right and into a pile of sand. No shot. Then Cloag started up again. As he repeated the same message we moved fast, keeping low in case we showed up against the moonlit buildings behind us in Basset Street. Then Cloag changed the wording.

'This is Detective Inspector Cloag. You are surrounded. Come out with your hands up.' The change meant nothing to the gunman but it meant a lot to us. If the gunman did not respond this time Bone and I would have to stay put until dawn. We had reached the limit of risk allowed us.

The silence dragged on. Then someone began to move at the back of the site. I raised my pistol. Somewhere to my left Bone was doing the same thing. Although we had split we were both well to the left of the site. Unless the gunman crept along the base of the wall and trod on Sergeant Bone he would have to pass to the right of both of us. There was no danger of Bone and I shooting each other. But would he come this way? We believed he would if only because the narrow back exit was blocked up by the patrol car.

Just ahead of me bricks were knocked off the edge of a stack. There was a muffled curse. Muffled? Had he hoped to conceal his advance? I held my pistol rock steady, knowing I was going to use it.

Cautious footsteps coming toward me. Cautious because he couldn't see? I didn't think so. It must be now! Now! He appeared towering over me against the night sky.

That was the moment Bone tapped several times on his radio; an unmistakable signal. In Basset Street the car lights came on. Another car swung up to the wire, headlights blazing. In the archway behind the gunman the unlit car began to roll forward.

Our man stood transfixed in the headlights as we crouched in the shadows to his left. He still had his gun.

'Drop the gun!' I yelled.

I was close enough, and the spotlights on him were bright enough, for me to see the shock spreading over his white face. He must have had no idea we were inside the wire. He began to turn raising the shotgun.

Bone and I probably fired together but the echoes merging with the shots made that difficult to confirm. The gunman lurched sideways, the gun slipping down and away from him. He toppled over and rolled onto his face. By the time the body had come to rest Bone and I had thrown ourselves into new hiding places. But no one fired at us.

'Come in,' said Bone into his radio, a slight tremor in his voice.

Cars swung in through both gates, headlights glaring. Men came running past and into the corners of the site. 'All clear!' shouted someone.

'You go, Jack!' said Bone.

'He's dead,' I said, standing beside the body, the shotgun under my foot. Bone lowered his pistol, came and stood beside me.

'You all right?' said Cloag, breathless, and not just from running. He knew what sort of risk he had asked us to take.

'He still had the gun,' I said. 'He turned it on us.'

'Shots fired?' asked Cloag.

'One, sir,' I said.

'One, sir,' said Bone.

'Who is he?' Shocked, I recognized

Green's voice. She was standing with Shalvin in the gateway. Why the devil had he brought her with him? I bent down, turned the heavy dead head to the side.

'Never seen him before,' I said.

'Nor me,' said Bone.

'Sure?' said Shalvin, foolishly. Neither of us had time to reply.

'Over here, sir! Over here!'

We clustered in a shocked bedraggled knot and looked down at the disturbed earth of the shallow grave. The hand that protruded from it was discoloured and appeared to be stretching for the spade that lay at the graveside. The fingers were splayed but not entirely limp.

'You did interrupt them, didn't you, Buttle?' said Cloag.

'Looks like it, sir,' said Buttle, smugly.

'No,' I said. 'Not really.'

'What do you mean?' said Cloag. 'Look at it! Grave filled in but hand sticking out. And you say he didn't interrupt them?'

'That's right, sir. Buttle interrupted their getaway but not the burial.'

'Oh, dear,' said Green. I looked sourly at her face, pale and gaunt in the headlights. Trust her to spot what was going on.

'Explain,' said Shalvin.

'If you and I were digging a grave, sir, surely we'd push the arm to the bottom first before filling in. Or if I said to you — 'Go and turn the van round while I finish off here' — I wouldn't say that with a hand still sticking out would I?'

'Only if you meant to leave the hand sticking out,' said Green. Someone sighed heavily.

'Why are we meant to find the body here, Jack?' asked Shalvin.

'I bet when we look at the builder's board facing onto Basset Street it says 'A, F and Z Builders'.'

'It does. I noticed that when I was waiting for you to arrive,' said Buttle. My colleagues shuffled themselves into a narrow triangle with me at the apex. I saw several mouths opening but got in first.

'Did you authorize a Press release about Tremayne's death for our evening newspaper, sir?'

'Dammit, I did,' said Shalvin.

'And A, F and Z Builders is a firm for

which Tremayne is a — was a director,' I said.

'But I still don't — ' began Cloag.

'Look,' said Shalvin. 'As a result of reading of his death someone decided to throw suspicion on Tremayne. This is how. Left a body on one of his building sites. Very clumsy but I see it's keeping a lot of us preoccupied.' Feet were shuffled but Cloag pressed on.

'Who's in — ' said Cloag, pointing at the spread hand.

'Anna Duras,' I said, sharply. 'The girl. The nice fresh corpse they hadn't had time to conceal properly.'

'Soon find out,' said Shalvin. 'Are Scene of Crime here yet?'

'Yes, sir,' said Cloag.

'Get 'em busy!' snapped Shalvin. 'And I want a word with you, Inspector!' It was Cloag's turn to shuffle his feet. 'Now you all know what to do,' said Shalvin, loudly. 'Do it! I want Sergeant Bone and DC Bull in my car.'

As I turned away from the sad, imploring hand I came face to face with Green.

166

'Black magic,' I said.

'What do you mean?' she asked, defensively.

'Three years with no bodies, then three days with you and I've got three of 'em. Who's next — one of us?' I waved a heavy arm at my colleagues.

'Come on, Jack. Leave it alone,' said Bone, like myself unaware of my new-found powers of prophesy.

'Last day of carnival. Congratulations on the timing,' I said to no one in particular.

Bone and I walked to Shalvin's car, sat in the back seat together. The driver stood some ten yards away, perhaps because he was a tactful soul. There was no need for words between Bone and myself; each could feel the other shaking. No pretence. Killing a man kills a bit of yourself.

I watched Shalvin and Cloag walking to the car. They stopped a few feet away. Shalvin must have known we had the windows down on so warm a night. He did not lower his voice.

'What the bloody hell did you think you were doing?' he said, icily.

'I thought it important — ' began Cloag.

'You thought? You never thought at all. You sent those two in there in darkness, not even sure how many gunmen there were, and you say you thought!'

'Excuse me, sir, it was — '

'This'd better be good, Inspector, bloody good. At the moment it just looks like you'd do anything for a bit of glory.'

'That's not fair, sir,' said Cloag, looking shiftily in our direction. He also knew the car windows were open.

'What is then?' said Shalvin.

'Bone and Bull had quite explicit orders about how far to go into the site if the gunman resisted.'

'Why didn't you wait for daylight?'

'The high wire fence, sir. I wanted to be sure that if we had to wait I already had marksmen inside the site before daybreak. It would've been almost impossible to get over that wire or through that gateway without casualties in daylight.' *If Cloag's premise was right he had actually conducted the operation very well but I wouldn't be saying so.*

'But why do that anyway? Why couldn't we have waited it out?' Shalvin's voice shook.

'I didn't think time was on our side, sir.'

Yes, I thought, with the Yard due down here this was Cloag's last fling. Shalvin followed a slightly different tack.

'I daresay you can make it all sound feasible — to yourself, Inspector. But one unfortunate result of your haste is that we have an unidentified dead man in there. None of us know him.'

'In my briefing I specifically stated the importance of getting him alive, sir.'

'Yes,' said Shalvin, slowly. 'I'm sure you did. But it wasn't at you that the shotgun was pointed.' Cloag completely misunderstood the remark.

'No, sir. This is the second time in less than twenty-four hours that DC Bull's been involved in the shooting of a vital witness.'

I must have made a sudden movement because Bone clamped his hand on my arm. I looked at him and saw his shoulders rise and fall in a shrug identical to the one he had made when Cloag announced we were going to get the gunman off the site.

Shalvin got into the car without looking at us, then looked out at Cloag. 'You're in charge here. Clear up your own mess!'

# 14

'You didn't get back to bed last night?' asked Green as we got into her car outside the station.

'No. Shooting someone makes a bit of paperwork!' She ignored my anger.

'Sir Bertie's kept it all out of the newspapers,' she said. I made no reply. 'So tell me the news, Jack. Was it Anna Duras in the grave?'

'Yes. Throat cut. At least, that's what the Doc. chose.'

'What's that supposed to mean?'

'Done so savagely it was almost decapitation.'

'Hmmm.' She started the car, swung round the corner. 'That could mean someone or something is still heavily blood-stained.'

'Maybe. Time of death almost certainly Saturday night or early Sunday. Time to

171

clean up. She was dead before you and I even met.'

'Sexually assaulted?'

'No.'

'And who was the burial party?'

'Henry John Bishop. CRO turned him up. Long record of minor offences, none in Clapton: petty thieving mostly.'

'Hardly big league was he? Right out of his depth this last and final time.'

'Makes you wonder about the van driver. Big boss got away and left the hireling in the lurch.'

'Could be. But let's not start bloody speculating. The facts we know are confusing enough.'

'Yeah. And as that sod, Cloag was quick to point out I've now shut the mouth of another useful witness.'

'Stop feeling sorry for yourself. No need to whine about Cloag! You and I can manage without him.'

'We can?'

'Where did Bishop come from?' she said, firmly.

'Plout. It's a village the other side of Harmsworth, twenty-five miles away.'

'That's almost abroad by Clapton standards. Maybe he hadn't realized what he'd got himself into.'

'Likely. Anyway, all his contacts'll be thoroughly turned over today. Chief Inspector Richardson will handle all that. Shalvin's decided you and I don't have to bother about that part of the investigation.'

'Good. We can concentrate on meeting your blackmailing suspect.'

'Yes. Take the next turn left.'

'And how *is* Shalvin?' she asked. 'Sir Bertie got him by the short and curlies because of yesterday's Press release about Tremayne's death?'

'Hardly — since he approved it. Anyway, Shalvin'd not be much bothered by that. He's too busy making one last desperate effort to crack this case. Partly explains why almost anything goes! Success means retirement in glory. Failure underlines the fact he's been on this case three years already. Worst of all, from his point of view now, is that we might have made sufficient progress to enable his successor to clean up. Looks bad if a new man succeeds where he failed.'

'He thinks you're right about Tremayne being something of a red herring?'

'Not a red herring exactly. Tremayne must've been directly involved to some degree. We can't keep dismissing evidence that points at him — even if it is circumstantial and/or manufactured. There's his suicide during an interview, evidence of blackmail, possibly some quirkiness in his private life, and now a body on the building site being worked by one of his companies.'

'And in our interview with him he made no complaint about building work being held up by police action.'

'Right, Susie. Not sure what it all means but Tremayne's in there somewhere and not smelling of violets. The only thing we know he did *not* do was bury Anna Duras. But he could certainly have killed her. The latest she died was Sunday lunch time, and Tremayne didn't shoot himself until Monday afternoon.'

'Suddenly, we're on the edge of solving this, aren't we?'

'Perhaps. Stop here.'

She braked unnecessarily hard. I was not the only one feeling bad-tempered. Why was she cross? I had the feeling it was not something to do with the case. Dismayed, I considered the awful mistake I might have made. Her cool smile on being rejected last night might have hidden more than chagrin at a ploy that failed. Had she wanted to sleep with me for herself, as it were, and not merely as a part of her investigation of me? Not even my arrogance had led me to consider that possibility. Yet up on Hangman's Moor. And last night I'd jumped out of her car like an affronted virgin! It was possible that almost my only piece of 'correct behaviour' had been an error of judgement. God! The real illogicality of feminine logic is man's struggle to live with it. But too late now.

We left the car on the lane above Granny Hemyock's place and walked down the hill through the woods. Despite the shade of the trees we were soon perspiring.

'Here we are,' I said, breathlessly.

We stood inside the cool black, blue-black wood and looked out across field and track to Granny Hemyock's cottage lying snug against the far hillside. To the left, beyond the cottage and across another grass field, lay the crinkled cliff edge and the haze-swathed Channel drifting into a milky sky. A world suspended in heat.

'So very quiet.' Green spoke slowly as if reluctant to grind up the breathless silence.

'Yes — and isolated. There's a dangerous footpath down the cliff, and the track from the front of the cottage is the only road to town.'

'Suppose we'd better go out into the sun and call on the old lady,' she said, regretfully. 'What's the time?'

'09.20. But wait,' I said, grasping her arm. (First touch of the day.) 'Tell me what you see from here.' She shook herself free of me before answering.

'A timber and plaster cottage, thatched roof spoilt by patching, set tight in the hillside with a back garden ending at the foot of a steep slope. In front the land slopes this way and the small front garden is full of flowers. The fence is broken down on both sides of the front gate. Then there's the field with the track leading to town, then the edge of this wood.'

'Now for the first of several nasty surprises,' I said, leading the way forward. And she, expecting only the shock of the heat, was doubly shocked. On each side of us, but hidden by the wood until we emerged, stood great mounds of scrap metal: wrecked cars, rusted machinery, even a shattered bus; smaller objects, memorials of daily living — mangles, dustbins, baths, broken bedsteads, light switches, old wiring, burnt-out saucepans. 'Terrible, ain't it?' I said.

'And Granny and her friends look out at this mess every day?'

'They scrape a living off this muck in winter then batten on town and tourists like summer leeches with jobs as bouncers, buskers, procurers, pickpockets. All got some form except Granny.'

'And Granny is boss?'

'Yes. Problem is why? Could understand it if she was expert at robbing banks, say. They'd bow to her superior skills. But it's some other hold she's got.'

'So she's chief villain but has no form. I don't like that, Jack. Not even for a gang as petty as you say this lot is. A boss who's clean always spells trouble of some kind. Any other women up here?'

'Only that dreamy girl you saw in the procession. Claims she's Granny's great-niece but no proof of course. They're worse than gypsies. Trouble is they never move on!'

'You don't really believe we'll get anything from them on this case?'

'We tried every time a girl disappeared. Blank faces, expressions of regret. You might do better because you're new. Can't do worse.'

'But your nose leads you back here every time, Jack?'

'That or false optimism based on the belief they know everybody's business. This time it was your question about a cool-headed blackmailer that made me think of Granny.'

'Herself or someone she knows of?'

'Your guess. But here we are. In case

she's watching pretend the fence is still standing and use the gate.'

'She has got you going, hasn't she?'

'Shut up and admire the garden.'

'Mad keen on poppies, isn't she?'

'She's a reputation as a herbalist. And you can't stop people growing single poppies in ornamental beds. She boasts she's got every single variety that will grow in Britain.'

'I can believe it. Everything's quiet, can we sneak a look round the back?'

'I'd prefer not.'

'Pull yourself together, Jack! We can always say we were admiring the garden or just looking for her.'

We trod like thieves round the side of the cottage. Nervously, I waited at the corner of the building. I was uneasy not so much because we were trespassing but because of where we were trespassing. I pretended I was standing in the shade. Green walked slowly along the uneven brick path that led through the garden to the hillside soaring above the cottage. I had the absurd idea that as she walked toward the hill a door would open and she would vanish into the ground. The garden was alien to me somehow. Ever since I had first seen it, it had been a place for man-eating rhubarbs and plants unbearably slimy to the touch. I watched Green brushing past oddly-shaped plants that swayed over the path as if to detain her. The frantic happiness of the bees, the fragrancies of plants spoke of a well-stocked herb garden. But the subtleties of scents, of growth, of uses of herbs were transmuted into murky secrets simply because it was Granny Hemyock's garden. I sighed with relief when Green returned to the cottage. Knowing I was being stupid made no difference to my feelings. Does it ever?

'You a gardener?' she whispered, perhaps more affected by the atmosphere than she would admit.

'Not a clue. Ask Dan Thirkettle about gardening.'

'Hmm. Nightshade, Wolf's Bane, Laburnum, Mandrake — Blimey! herbs. You know?'

The shock of an explosion almost lifted us off the ground. Sweat bursting we turned. Granny Hemyock leaned her stumpy body against the wall and cackled at us, the burst paper bag still held in her dark claws. 'Made you jump, did I? Serves you right. Trespassers!'

We stared at her. Green stopped fumbling in her handbag. I was frozen in my own sweat. Granny looked me up and down, her lip curling. She peered more closely at Green and her expression changed. The split paper bag fell from her hands.

'Who's this?' she hissed at me.

'Detective Sergeant Green.'

'And your woman? Why bring her to me? I cannot heal your differences. Or have you come to make things right for yourselves before you bring in those big machines again, tearing up my ground again?'

I was not given time to reply.

'You're Granny Hemyock,' said Green, in a strange voice. 'I should have brought a sprig of garlic.'

'Clever bitch!' Granny pointed a finger at her. 'You and I must talk, must we? Bring the boy into the house with you.'

'What — ?' I said, weakly.

'Shut up!' whispered Green. 'Just look and listen, for God's sake. And don't bloody leave me with her!'

We blundered into the dark house and into an almost empty room. Expecting clutter and squalor, Green was obviously surprised by the spartan furnishings: a close-spaced group of hard upright chairs in the centre and a great wooden chest against one wall. Nothing else. The grey walls were bare, the grate empty. Only the gleaming floorboards and shining small windows betrayed affectionate hands. But it was a cold room.

'Lucky to see this room,' said Granny. 'I usually puts visitors, 'specially unwelcome visitors, in the kitchen. But some of my boys are sleeping off a heavy breakfast and a hard night. Sit facing me, girl. You boy, this chair on my left.'

We sat silent. Granny's walnut face almost vanished in the gloom. Her eyes were black pits. I did not think it absurd that evil secrets might have been voiced in the low, dark room.

'You be silent, young Jack!' snapped

Granny. I was not so startled as Green. Having dealt with the old woman before I knew she enjoyed making unexpected remarks; enjoyed the effect created if, by chance, they were appropriate to the other person's thoughts. It enhanced her reputation as a mind-reader. I was not much impressed by that side of her.

'You see I have no black cat?' This to Green who jerked in her chair. 'Ha!' said Granny, honour satisfied.

'I need your help,' said Green, firmly.

'Aye. But your troubles are beyond my helping.'

'But not all of them. You can help me because you know this town, the people.'

'But this is nothing to you,' said Granny. There was another silence. 'Finding missing girls is nothing to you. You are after another prey.'

'No!' exclaimed Green. For an instant I had the feeling Granny and I were temporarily on the same side.

'Give me your hand!' commanded Granny. We knew she was not about to read palms. They held hands, the two women; the young and old, the lovely and raddled; but both malevolent. I had the uncomfortable feeling Granny wanted me to see Green in the same light as I saw her. Two witches? Granny turned and scowled at me. I bit back my words. She turned back to Green.

'We both know evil,' she said to her suppliant. 'Pah! You reek of it! Yet you are still young and ignorant. Your hands are not scarred but who marked your head?' Green half-raised her other hand but her wig had not slipped. 'Give me some credit,' said Granny, sharply.

After several minutes of silence Granny released her hand. 'What help from me?'

'About a man,' said Green in a high voice. 'A man who may know what happened to a girl three years ago.'

'Should I know of every little man?'

'He is not a little man. Did you read of his death in the newspaper?'

'Oh — him. Yes, but should I say he is innocent and cause suspicion to fall on others? Should I say his guilt was as you imagine it and condemn him for wrong causes? The man we think of now was a fool.'

'But he was not a murderer?'

'Should I help you, you so clever police?'

'If you are innocent yourself.'

'Which you know I am not. How can a woman of my age be *innocent* of anything?'

'Of blackmail, of murder?' I whispered.

'Ha! You ask the wrong questions, boy. You can think only of people in terms of *your* law. You and I can never talk for long, boy. We've tried before but there's no bridge between us. You have an official mind. This woman, your woman is different. She has enjoyed what would make you guilty. She could be a believer. Not you!' The last two words were uttered with stinging contempt.

I wanted to spring up, could not stir. 'You feel my words now in your bones?' asked Granny, more gently. I did not reply.

'And you girl — beware false answers. The answers you dream up. He was guilty but not of murder. For murder he would have paid an even greater price. Seek your other answers in some other places. I'm no informer, no creeping Jesus. No more help from me. Go!'

We stood up and Green raised her hand to her breast as if to cross herself. Granny Hemyock opened her eyes very wide. 'No need,' she said. 'No need. Your crown of thorns is enough. You have marked my days.' With this cryptic comment Granny closed her eyes, slumped back on her chair. We left her in her bare room.

'Old charlatan,' I whispered, unconvincingly, as I opened the front door.

Outside under the porch, apparently sheltering from the sun, stood Snoad and Greening. They stepped just far enough apart to allow us to squeeze between them.

'Miss Green, I assume,' said Greening. 'Will our names keep us close?'

'And how do you know my name?' she demanded.

'As everyone does: gossip and chat, gossip and chat.'

'And you think I should know yours?'

'You do, Miss, I'm sure.'

'Excuse us,' I said, irritably.

We plunged into the sunlight as if hoping the brilliance would cleanse. 'Ugh!' said Green. 'Very nasty. And they smell horrible!'

I said nothing but strode ahead of her. The whole world was mad. And since when did DS Green belong to the Catholic Church? Cross yourself! I couldn't let that pass.

'She really had you going, didn't she?' I probably sounded sulky but didn't care. 'Even crossing yourself!'

'Do what?' She looked at me with that wide-eyed stare that made me want to slap her face. 'You're as big a fool as Granny. I was scratching my sunburn!'

'Oh.' Temporary collapse of tired party, collapsed but not necessarily convinced. I stopped and she nearly collided with me. We turned and looked back at the house; friendly in the sun, sparkling windows opening into shady rooms, the tattered thatch adding an air of rakish good humour. In the doorway Snoad's skull shone comically like a porch light.

'The gingerbread house or how Hansel and Gretel escaped the black witch,' I muttered, wiping my face with a handkerchief.

'But I think the children will have to come back,' said Green. 'That witch is more than just a silly old woman. And a scrap heap's a convenient place to hide a body.'

'Give us credit for some sense,' I said. 'Even we worked that out. Moved the lot with a bulldozer last year.' My anger was directed at her but was also a response to being in a situation I did not understand. Something significant had passed between Green and Granny Hemyock and I had been excluded from the transaction. 'No point moving the scrap this year. We've got Anna's body.'

'Yes and that's exactly *why* we move it. Someone might've thought to move some stale corpses while we're distracted by a fresh one. And I'll tell you this for free. You could be right about Granny. She's mad enough and cunning enough to have blackmailed a rich man and not increased the take more than once. There are several reasons for coming back again!'

# 15

Without speaking, Green drove the Mini back into Clapton. I did not ask what else she suspected after visiting Granny Hemyock. I glanced sideways at my chauffeuse. She appeared to be very much on edge, as if the visit had caused her some kind of personal distress. She was bursting to reveal a troubling and possibly discreditable idea. My interpretation of her condition was temporarily replaced by a more prosaic explanation.

'Jack, can we stop off at your place? I'm dying to go to the loo.'

'You're the driver.'

'Sorry but I'm bursting.'

'Spare me the details. Just make sure we reach Sir Bertie's place by midday, that's all.'

Opening my front door I stepped aside but she half-waved, half-pushed me ahead

189

of her. On the landing she opened her bag.

'Don't bother,' I said. 'Leave the penny 'til later.' In the instant of uttering the feeble joke I knew she had deceived me again. She did not need to pull out the pistol, her face was weapon enough. It bore the same expression as last night when I had slammed her car door in her face outside my flat.

'Inside!' she said, the pistol rock steady. I stepped back, half-turning, half-stumbling into my sitting-room.

Two men sat on my settee. In front of one — Abe's 'Duke of Wellington' — stood my coffee table covered with documents. But it was immediately apparent that his gigantic coarse-featured companion was the man in charge. Now I knew to whom Green had been speaking on her radio. Almost blind with rage I heard myself shouting, heard replies, dimly saw the spare key held up in explanation: borrowed by DS Green. At the mention of her name the giant orchestra in my head ceased tuning, fell silent awaiting a conductor. I expressed the opinion I would like to sit down, fell into the armchair furthest from the settee. Green stood just behind me. She *had* had a troubling and discreditable secret after all.

'Good morning, DC Bull,' said the coarse-featured man. He sounded like a child's dream of God.

'My chief, Mr Frimmer,' said Green, deferentially.

I said nothing. Many things were about to be explained including her deference.

Frimmer dominated the room even when sitting down. He was a heavily muscled man just beginning to run to fat; any age between forty and sixty. His large, close-cropped head was square and decorated with small ears apparently stuck on cold after birth. Absence of neck was understandable. Such a head could only be a direct extension of the shoulders. Facially, he was even more unattractive having apparently acquired his features from stock for spare part surgery. The result: big-eyed, porcine.

'Mr Stone,' he said, without taking his eyes off me. The man beside him momentarily emerged from the flowered pattern of the loose covers, nodded his aristocratic head, shifted papers with his left hand. His right hand rested in his pocket. That pose had been commented on before. He and Frimmer together frightened the shits out of me. No wonder Green was so respectful. Frimmer smiled coldly and drew a cigar from his pocket.

'Don't smoke in my home,' I said, weakly.

Frimmer lit up, drew in reflectively, exhaled. He looked round the room. 'Nice place, Bull. You'll be sorry to leave.' I dug my nails into the arms of the chair. Nothing but nothing was going to make me rise to that sort of remark. 'It seems,' said Frimmer, with grating good humour, 'that the case you are on is complex. Could you possibly conclude the whole dreary business this week? No opinion? Well, how about you, Green?'

'Sir. The local force is giving maximum effort and although DC Bull is exhausted —'

'Who says I'm exhausted?'

'Come off it, Jack. You nearly broke down the other morning when I wore

Jeannie's apron. Why d'you think I suggested we lie about on the moor?' She was a real butcher with her little knife.

'Can we get on?' snarled Frimmer. 'Believe it or not she's again reporting in your favour, Bull.'

'I was going to say he's made some progress over Tremayne and also has suspicions about the Hemyock woman as a possible blackmailer. He may be right.'

'Agreed, Bull?' Long pause. 'Look, sonny, I only call assistant commissioners 'sir' — and that's only when I'm in a good mood or want something.'

'And I'm even fussier,' I said, shortly.

The silence that followed was accompanied by a strange vibration within the settee. It was several seconds before I realized Frimmer was laughing silently.

'Stone and I are not lurking in your home from choice. Where else in Clapton could we have a confidential chat with you without anyone else knowing about it?'

'Then say your piece and go. And take her with you!'

'Good for you,' said Frimmer, falsely

admiring. 'I'll be brief. I want you to come and work for me and my department. You have no family ties, you're young, tough, quite intelligent, a marksman, an experienced junior CID man. Your colleagues will be pleased to see you move on because they hate your guts.'

'That's not — '

'Shut up and don't blether! You're not liked because you're public school, you've got money and, worst of all, you're a pushy little sod. But I *like* pushy little sods, especially when they've learnt to push in the right direction.'

'And which direction's that?'

'Toward any villains Mr Stone can unveil for us.' He made a gesture as if dragging them out of the pockets of his crumpled, overtight suit. 'We're not too bothered by the rule book so I'm offering a job right up your street.'

I stayed silent, still burning at the remark about my colleagues. But I was interested, very interested.

'It's quite legal,' said Frimmer, misunderstanding my silence. 'Chief Superintendent

Shalvin will vouch for me.'

'He knows about this?'

'In outline.'

'And the Chief Constable?'

'Dear me, no. Don't want him telling his fellow chief constables to look out for that nasty Mr Frimmer who poaches young policemen. I've enough recruiting problems as it is. He won't stand in your way though — once he gets your formal application. He's more than a little embarrassed by the frequency with which you bring in your man damaged. Too many broken limbs, noses, etc. He fears you are a vicious young yob. Doubtless, he is right. No, Shalvin's my man down here. First, he doesn't care much about future staffing — he's retiring. Second, I did the old boy a favour once when his feet nearly slipped on the promotion ladder.'

Even Shalvin has his price, I thought. And so have I. 'Why pick on me?' I asked.

'No one else has your record, that's for sure! And who else would've taken DS Green with a toy pistol? Ha!' Frimmer slapped his fat thigh.

'But it wasn't quite like that. It — '

'Don't blether! It happened. You did it. *And* you're still alive to argue about it. I like your style. I also like the fact you're short and swarthy, more like a gypsy than a copper. That could be useful.'

'But why get onto me in this underhand way?'

'I'm only allowed to recruit from the police and some sections of the armed services. I need a helluva lot of back-ground information on a man before I approach him, and I need to be discreet. How the hell d'you think I can get suitable staff otherwise? Work my way along queues for James Bond films?'

I lay back in my chair. Listening was free and did no harm. Some of his misinterpretations were comical.

'I'm offering you, Bull, much more interesting work with salary at least a rank above your present one plus exceptional promotion prospects. My department is concerned with the job of unearthing crime and not just catching criminals. For example, last year we helped local police forces re-open seventeen cases of accidental death that could have been murder.

This led to prosecutions in six of those cases. Get the idea?'

'A version of the Serious Crimes Squad?'

'Not quite. More the Suspected Serious — the S.S. I quite like that!'

Yes, I thought, you would. I can guess what you'd've become if Hitler had won. Not surprising Abe smelt you out so quickly. 'But why a separate outfit?'

'Obvious. First, a local force may not be too keen on looking under the larger stones or opening up old, half-forgotten files. Not being the Yard we don't wait for invitations, we sneak in. Second, not all policemen are straight, are they? We're looking forward to the day we can investigate A10! That'll mean we've really arrived!'

'I can see how some of this relates to Clapton but what's she got to do with it?' I jerked my head back at Green, could not speak her name.

'DS Green has given you an excellent report.'

'That's nice.' The bitterness in my voice silenced Frimmer for a moment. He stared above my head at Green. She did not speak.

Many things were being explained. *This* was why I had been put to work with her, was why our relationship had continued off-beat, why we refuged in an uneasy kind of humour. No point in telling Frimmer she might be mad; he knew her better than I did. Perhaps it was now clear why she would not report to Shalvin in front of Cloag. Perhaps it explained why she lurked in the alleyway on Carnival Night. Perhaps it didn't. I asked.

'That wasn't me,' she said, in a strained voice. There was a moment of silence.

'Interesting,' said Frimmer. 'Follow that up some time, Bull. Meantime accept my offer.'

But I was still lurching back through the past. 'Suppose this explains why you kept out of my way the first few days you were down here. And there was I wondering if you'd been having it off with Slinfield!'

'Idiot!' She stepped from behind my chair, stood looking down at me, no sign of the pistol. 'You think the oddest things about me.'

'You've said that before and it's been justified before. Finding these two freaks in my home justifies anything I choose to think about you.'

'Oh,' said Frimmer, softly. 'Bitter are we? Could it be — ?' He paused, stared again at Green. 'Susie, my dear, you haven't got yourself emotionally involved? Oh dear. I'm surprised — and rather ashamed of you. You can't be quite as well as the doctors said.'

'And then some!' I said, viciously. 'But then anything goes for the Recruiting Sergeant!' Yet, oddly, my spirits lifted at that moment. Maybe my disgust, distrust were misplaced. Perhaps she really had — . But did it matter now? In a short time together she had involved me in just about every human emotion except one. Now it was too late, over. We were merely colleagues.

'Green is now going to telephone your chief constable,' explained Frimmer. 'She'll say you're unwell again and can't get to the interview but that she'll come instead. All helps to weaken resistance to your transfer.'

'I think you've already succeeded enough in that direction,' I said, calmly. I was surprised by the diminution of my rage. Perhaps I already knew that my future was with Frimmer.

'Off you go, dear,' said Frimmer, spitefully. 'Phone from a box, not from here. We've more talking to do.'

Green half-raised a hand toward me, her gesture when I arrived at the quarry. Then she walked out. I sat listening for the last time to her footfalls on my stairs, remembering how I had felt afraid when I first met her.

# 16

'So much for *my* young lady,' said Frimmer, harshly. 'Now let's talk about *your* ladies. It's the sort of case we specialize in, and happy coincidence we're recruiting you at the same time. We've a way of making things happen, haven't we?'

'But this could've broken without you,' I said, hoping to puncture his smugness.

'You think? When did it blow?'

'Tremayne's suicide.'

'Right. And who was with him?'

'DS Green. But — '

'Why 'but'? You'll never know what she really said to him, will you?' He said this with a kind of slimy satisfaction. Horrified, I stared at the creature.

'That's shut him up,' said Frimmer. 'Seems we've established our credentials, Stone. Now let's chew the fat. First, these

201

abducted girls had few or no friends. So *if* they had been taken by someone they *knew* then even your Force would've found out.' I nodded, ignored the sarcasm. 'So it's likely that the person or persons responsible were complete strangers to the girls. That's so even in the case of Tremayne's girl. Your colleagues have now checked back that he dropped her in town, and they've checked where he went and who he was with later that same evening. He couldn't've spent more than a few minutes in Clapton with her. This brings us to a vital question. Under what circumstances do girls go off with strangers?'

'At carnivals and parties?'

'Yes and no, sarky. Girls are likely to be on their guard then, aren't they?'

'Suppose so.'

'And at least one girl had a strongly religious cum moral background?'

'They often fall first.'

'A point. Shaky but a point.' Frimmer pulled at his left ear. Rather surprisingly it did not come off in his hand. 'How would *you* soften up a strange and suspicious female so that she did as you said, made no fuss, remained inconspicuous in her behaviour?'

'Drugs,' I said. 'Or careful application of drink — wouldn't want her giggling or vomiting.'

'Preference?'

'Drugs. Drink is more difficult to judge when pouring it into a stranger — and people notice what you're at. Big problem is getting the drug into the woman — perhaps in a harmless drink like fizzy lemonade. No problem obtaining drugs these days. Tell your GP you can't sleep.'

'I'll buy that idea,' said Frimmer. 'Now, the second thing is related to the first. If the villains don't know the girls what do they need to be sure they pick girls without friends?'

'Information?'

'Yes — just like us, like any police force, they need information. How did they get it?'

'Watching. Perhaps asking a few questions?'

'Who would they ask?'

'Employers, fellow-workers. Not many

other people to ask. I doubt they'd risk chatting up the girls until the night they pounced.'

'Who can snoop or call without arousing too much interest?'

'Gas man, Electricity — '

'Hang on. There's a snag, two snags. One is they'd have to call at several other houses to allay suspicion. The other is that someone might check back to the Gas Board for some reason. Then your local police might get called in. How about social workers?'

'Ye-es. And odd-jobbers, window cleaners, rag and bone men.'

'Second-hand clothing dealer?' said Mr Stone, unexpectedly.

'You mean Abraham Gretz?' I tried not to sound worried.

'Why not?' said Frimmer. 'D'you think being your grass makes him pure as snow? I bet he learned a lot about killing in the camps. He might be using *you* to find out if the police are on to him. Better leave Mr Gretz to us. We'll check him out.' He smirked horribly.

'He's spotted you two.'

'No matter. I think pressure is called for at this stage. And don't forget there's a bonus for you if we make quite sure he's in the clear.'

'What's that?'

'Don't be thick! If he's in the clear so are you. It means it was not *your* grass hoodwinking the local Force and not *you* being pumped for information. Now then, Bull, anyone else you can think of?'

'Milkman — but same snag as gasman. Scrap metal deal — . Oh, I like that one. Dear old Granny Hemyock. I think DS Green's arranging for us to turn over Granny's scrap heaps later today. Now there's a possibility!'

'So. Feel you might be warm?'

'Er — yes. Something there. Maybe she is more than a blackmailer.'

'Right. You can pick up that thread this afternoon. Any other suggestions?' He gave me a look. I knew they were going to hit me hard with something but I could never have prepared myself for the blow.

'Social workers?' said Stone.

'You've already mentioned — ' Then I stopped, looked from face to face. 'Oh,

Christ! You trying to say something about Jeannie? She was a social worker. What are you saying?'

'Don't shout,' growled Frimmer. 'We're not accusing her. Got that? But think about this idea carefully. Where does her death fit into the time scale of the disappearances?'

'Oh — er — between the Chief Constable's girl, Pat Marsden, last year and the girl this last weekend. But how could Jeannie — ?'

'She had a visitor job, didn't she?' asked Frimmer.

'Yes. But — '

'Listen, boy. Suppose her visits took her across the path of the killers. Perhaps she met one of them coming down a garden path or in the street. Maybe they saw her around too often for their peace of mind. They've done away with the Chief Constable's girl by this time and they're a bit edgy because of the connection with Old Bill. Then this woman they keep tripping over gets engaged to a police-man: you. Worse, you're a detective with something of a reputation for success with crime and women. So they set her up. Hit and run on a dark wet night. End of doubts.'

'No!'

'Why not? And you were only engaged for a month. That's one week before the announcement appeared in the local paper — with identifying photo I might add, one week of panic, one week of planning the spot and time, and then in the last week — '

'Proof?'

'Not a scrap. But looked at *from a distance* the view is rather alarming.'

'You just trying to increase my commitment?' I didn't recognize my own voice.

'I'm flattered you think I'm that much of a bastard — but no. It's a serious suggestion I'm making. We take a very careful look at any mystery death where there's a policeman relative or friend.'

The three of us sat quiet in my sitting-room. Jeannie had chosen the soft covers, the curtains, the carpet. It was as if a fourth figure had entered the fiery furnace.

'Can I go on?' asked Frimmer, eventually.

'Yes.'

'My next remarks may also cause you some distress but they need to be made. Perhaps DS Green prepared the ground a bit here. You are also dependent on information, aren't you? But it seems in very short supply at the local level. Is it possible that lack of information may relate to lack of loyalty somewhere?'

'Possible.' His words were nailing together a scaffold out of vague presentiments and unspoken theories in other people's minds.

'If solving this case uncovers a bent policeman or two so much the better. You don't like the idea but who does? Better we snare our own. And you'd better face up to the fact your own neck might be at stake. Shut up! That's not an accusation. But you must be realistic, especially as you nearly had trouble like this once before with Cloag. Of course, it may be that lack of information is due to lack of information. But — '

Reluctantly, I nodded.

'On the other hand,' said Frimmer, 'some people might prefer a perfect whitewash. Nice but unlikely. Another thing: to dare to take away a girl this year suggests they might *know* they're in the clear over the Chief Constable's girl last year. And if they *know* who told 'em?'

'Or are they so crazy they don't think of being caught?'

'Good point, Bull. But it don't necessarily invalidate my question. And if I am right about Jeannie it looks as if they stop at nothing and nothing will stop them — except us cracking the case.'

'Yes.'

'Right. Let's move on. How do these crimes differ from the Yorkshire Ripper Murders?' He gave me a moment to think. 'Well come on, Bull. Green told you and Shalvin that the case can be described as fantastic.'

'Well — no bodies — until last night, anyway.'

'Even more fantastic?'

'The girls all vanished at the same time each year?'

'Yes, Bull.' Frimmer spoke very softly.

'Now take that fact a step further. What's the safest time to take a girl?'

'Er — I suppose after the procession has broken up, mixed in with the crowd and everybody is merry.'

'Maybe that was true one year. But not this year. Think again for *this* year.'

I turned my tired brain from side to side but nothing surfaced. Our policemen aren't so wonderful when worn out.

'For God's sake! It's as clear as the nose on your face. They know the police are after them but for some reason, we don't yet know, it has to be Carnival Night, when the police are on their toes. So what time do they choose? No? I'll have to tell him.' He said this to Stone, mockingly sad. 'They won't take her before the procession will they? Everything neat and tidy, police looking for the unusual. They won't take her after the procession, not with extra police all over the place and difficult to locate. No, they take her during the procession when every policeman has a fixed point or a fixed task to attend to.' Echo of Susie Green talking on the way back from

Hangman's Moor.

'But that means — . You're suggesting — '

'Yes, Bull. You're there at last. I'm suggesting they knew where you and your colleagues were stationed. They knew the unguarded spots — the killing grounds. And how did they know?'

'I suppose they could've been told by the same person who told them they were in the clear after taking Sir Bertie's girl.'

'Very likely. And all the info they needed this time was the name of a stretch of road which, although packed with people, was not covered by a policeman. There are never enough policemen! So — if they could arrange for their previously drugged victim to be in that locality — . Smooth aren't they?'

'Unbelievably.'

'All right, so I'm guessing. But why not try it for size until you can do better. And remember — they took the Chief Constable's girl and still didn't get touched. Imagine the effect of that on their informant, Bull; assuming he really knew what was going on. If he didn't then they could still feed him some line about wanting the information simply to help with a pick-pocketing scheme or some-thing. Sold him some tale he wanted, even *needed* to believe. As long as no body was found he could deceive himself. It's no more unlikely than the mother who believes her son innocent of murder even after the poor sod's pleaded guilty. But what's he going to believe now we do have a body?'

Frimmer scowled at me. 'Do some of these ideas fit?'

'Could do.' My reluctance to believe was partly horror at what a colleague had wittingly or unwittingly done, partly the unlikely nature of Frimmer's theories. Ironically, my disbelief was illustrating his argument.

'But now something's happened to panic them,' Frimmer was remorseless. 'I wonder what it was? Tremayne's death, perhaps? Or something to make them slit that girl's throat and leave us to find the body? Which of those events has really given us our break? Henry John Bishop might've told us had you and Bone been less good at your job.'

'Or Cloag not so bad at his,' said Stone, unexpectedly.

'Hmmm,' said Frimmer. 'Well let's leave it there for a few hours. Stone and I will go now. You'll continue to work with DS Green — on any personal basis you like. But you'll stay with her and she'll keep me informed of progress. And there will certainly be progress! No leads for years and suddenly — three bodies in the mortuary. Someone's panicky, Bull. I can almost smell the sweat!'

We all stood. Stone, using both hands to collect his papers, revealed that his right hand was a steel claw. Frimmer saw my face change.

'Yes, young Bull. I never said I was offering you a safe job, did I? And by the way — don't rely on that silly trick with bits of black cotton. We just put 'em back in place after we checked you out. We'll teach you some better dodges when you join us. Right, we're now going to see your know-all, kosher-all friend.'

'Just go easy there,' I said, angrily. 'He's

had enough griefs without you adding to them!'

'Me?' said Frimmer, spreading his hands, smiling oilily. 'Me, my dear?'

When they had gone I opened all the windows. In the last traces of cigar smoke I imagined I saw a frightened old man in a dark alley crouching pleadingly in front of Frimmer. But the old man's face was mine not Abraham's. I walked slowly into the kitchen. For a long time I stood staring out to sea.

# 17

As we climbed the hill to Granny's place I risked a quick glance at Dan walking beside me. He seemed greyer of face than could be explained by the short time spent walking in the dusty wake of the bulldozer. Before starting up the path he had complained at great length about the heat, the futility of this operation and about the previous year's unsuccessful search in Granny's scrap heaps. He had been more than just old-womanish about it. His complaints had been tinged with the desperation of a man forced into the path of some looming disaster. The expression on my face had eventually silenced him.

Behind us the bulldozer ground its way along the clifftop track churning up dust that billowed out behind it and spread like a greasy grey film above the town. The vivid yellow machine stood out against black storm clouds assembling over the sea. Dan and I had started the journey walking behind the machine but the choking dust had driven us to the front. I looked back at the driver perched high above us. Overalls and goggles had transformed someone familiar into a maniac who would pulp us under the tracks if we slowed down.

Whatever else I felt about DS Green I had to admit her efficiency. In the last four hours she had not only interviewed Slinfield she had also organized this search. It was easy to detract from her efforts by saying the exercise was simply a repeat of last year, but we *were* repeating it despite widespread pessimism about its outcome. I wondered if anything more useful would come from it than from her interview with Slinfield; an interview she had reported on in one word: useless. I realized I was walking along and shaking my head at the same time. It seemed appropriate.

I led my little procession into Granny Hemyock's field and past the line of police cars. The bulldozer stopped beside the first of the two great junk hills. Granny Hemyock was sitting in an old armchair outside the front gate of her cottage. Beside her stood Snoad. A few yards away, huddled together as if for mutual protection, stood Shalvin, Cloag, Bone and PC Buttle. Through the small windows of the tiny cottage I glimpsed uniformed men moving purposefully about their business. Granny's place was being very thoroughly turned over. As if to emphasize that thoroughness, Greening and Block were propelled violently out of the front door. Behind them, Green dusted off her hands and walked toward the bulldozer. 'You stay out!' she snarled over her shoulder. Embarrassed by the woman, Greening sniggered and Block nodded and bowed. As she walked toward me I sidled into the haven of Shalvin's little group.

PC Buttle waved an arm in the direction of the woods and twenty overalled constables emerged; some with spades, some with pick axes and some with metal rods. This dramatic development impressed everyone except Granny

Hemyock who gave a piercing yell of laughter and began rocking from side to side in her chair. Then, some-what hesitantly, Greening and Block began to smile and even Snoad allowed one corner of his mouth to twitch. My legs felt even weaker. It was all going to go wrong. Whatever Granny was up to it could not be buried under a scrap heap. I looked at my senior colleagues. Uneasiness showed on their faces. Shalvin turned on me.

'Afternoon, Bull,' he said, heavily. 'You managed *this* appointment at least.'

'Wasn't delayed by your one-armed bandit friend, sir.'

'Oh — I see. Say no more.' Shalvin looked quickly at the policeman nearest us. 'Discretion, Bull. Well, tell your driver to get on with it!'

I signalled to the bulldozer driver. Roaring, the machine advanced hungrily on the first pile of scrap; the pile with the old bus in the centre. The bulldozer grappled with the creaking, clattering mound. The noise was frightful. I jumped when Green lightly touched my shoulder. I had not heard her walk up behind me.

She put her mouth against my ear.

'There's something here, Jack. Not sure what but I'm even more convinced than before.'

Sullenly shrugging, I turned back to the scrap heap now shuddering under the repeated charges of the bulldozer. Suddenly, a large part of the heap gave way and the front of the bus was exposed for the first time. Then I was running, waving my arms at the bulldozer driver, screaming at him to stop. I nearly got myself crushed to death between a car chassis and a battered sink before the driver could slam on the brakes. The machine rocked in its tracks. Hearing shouts, pounding footsteps behind me, I looked back.

'What's up?' bellowed Shalvin and Cloag together.

'There's someone in the bus!'

The driver of the bulldozer switched off the engine. In the deafening silence we stared at the wreck. The old bus had finally died when its driver had taken a wrong turning and driven it under a low bridge. The top deck had been torn off leaving the jagged ends of the window frames pointing to the sky. Now there was a new driver in the cab, a figure indistinctly seen through filthy windows. I clambered toward the bus. At a distance of twenty feet I thought I recognized the man. 'Tremayne!'

'Rubbish!' said Shalvin, uncertainly.

Behind us Granny gave another great shriek of laughter. I pressed my face against the dirty glass. Staring eyes met mine. I felt my hair rising even as I realized the driver was a dummy. A crudely coloured death mask had been fitted to a life-size dummy made of old rags. The deception would not have fooled anybody at twenty yards in broad daylight, but crouched in the shadowed cab, viewed through dirty windows, and with Tremayne on everyone's mind, the dummy was enough to turn stomachs.

By the time we had dragged it from the cab Granny Hemyock had arrived at the base of the scrap heap. 'Mind my guy,' she cackled. 'W'm entering him for the com'tition in Town Park tonight. You knows — at the fireworks party.' She laughed so much Snoad had to bang her on the back. I hope that bloody hurt, I thought. The old bitch really had us going then. And we can't do anything about it. We'd be laughed out of court if we pretended she had obstructed us by storing a guy in a wrecked bus! Can't defeat laughter.

She was quite right about the competition. The guy judged to be the best would be placed on top of the great bonfire; the other entries placed lower down. The owner of the winning guy not only received first prize but was also invited to light the bonfire: the signal for the firework display to begin. I looked down at the guy. Now it looked nothing like Colonel Tremayne. Knowing Granny was watching me I deliberately kicked the body in the ribs. The effect was horrible. The flabby body jerked, twisted and assumed a position similar to that of the dead man in the quarry.

I stepped back, half-fell, half-lowered myself onto an upturned, rusty, perforated bucket. I hoped it was the heat making me fanciful. My companions were staring in astonishment at my white face. I stared back at them. Under the black sky the pride of my Force dripped perspiration and wobbled unsteadily on the rusting hill. Compared with Frimmer they were a whey-faced lot. Shalvin had one foot in a tin bath, Sergeant Bone was caught up in a bicycle wheel, Cloag was apparently relieving himself in a water tank, while PC Buttle had one leg caught in an old lavatory seat. Comical they were but no laughter came from me.

Then Green spoke, her words ripping over the jagged metal slope. 'They knew! They bloody knew!'

'Why not?' I said. 'It was in the papers.'

'No, fool! Not about Tremayne. They knew we were going to turn over the heaps.'

We all looked at Granny. She stopped cackling. For a moment she was just a frightened, shifty-eyed old woman.

'Go back to the house, Granny!' ordered Green.

As she turned to obey, her followers stepped away from her. The tension was heavier, more breathless than the encroaching storm. On the faces of Granny's men I saw defeat, despair. I knew then what had beaten them: a leader beyond their influence, outside their control, madly leading them to a blind drop at a cliff. This, her latest ploy, was the joke beyond a joke, laughter from a grave. As I watched them trail after her to the cottage I felt a rising excitement. Perhaps we *were* getting close. But Green was approaching the same conclusion from a different angle.

'Who told 'em?' she demanded.

'What d'you mean?' said Shalvin, sharply. 'Could be coincidence the dummy is here.'

'You reckon?' Green would not be deflected. 'That old woman knew precisely when we were launching this search, yet we only decided on the timing about three hours ago. So how did she know?' Silence. 'OK I can't prove it but didn't it seem to those of you who came here with me that we were expected?'

'Yes.' It was Sergeant Bone who spoke. 'At least — I'd say *she* was not surprised to see us,' he added, almost apologetically.

'Evidence?' Cloag drawled the word from the safety of the solid ground to

223

which he had retreated. 'After all we did search here last year. They would presumably expect a repeat this year.' Behind him the twenty men shuffled their spades and picks.

'Who knew of this operation earlier today?' Green asked the question as though Cloag had not spoken. It was Shalvin who broke first.

'You,' he said, 'me, Cloag, Bone, Thirkettle and Bull.'

'Who's your driver?' said Green, flatly. She pointed at the masked man perched on the bulldozer. Although he could not have heard the question at that distance, he obligingly removed his goggles revealing the innocent face of PC Piper. Someone sighed heavily. The implications of Green's words were sinking deeper.

'We'll think on it,' said Shalvin. 'But you keep your mouth shut. Right? Let's get on with this search!' What else could he have said? What difference would it have made anyway?

We found nothing. A long afternoon of bulldozing, of digging and probing, of searching house and garden a second time revealed nothing incriminating. And all the wasted effort was expended under the amused eyes of Granny Hemyock and her much less amused thugs. The young girl, Granny's great-niece, made mugs of herbal tea for the sweating constables but there was no way of telling if Block and his friends had spat in them first.

Most frustrating for me was the feeling we might be searching in the right place. Maybe it had nothing to do with the case of the missing girls but — . Head spinning, I wandered through the cottage garden. What the hell was it? I banged my forehead with my fists. Turning sharply, I nearly collided with the young girl. Blank-eyed, she stared at me as if the major part of her brain had been removed. Perhaps there was an affinity between us. Nervously, I stepped round her, fled the garden and went into Granny's sitting-room.

Granny Hemyock was sitting absolutely still on one of the hard, straight-backed chairs. Eventually, she turned her brown face toward me. We stared at each other. Unlike the girl, Granny had eyes clear and sharp enough. Neither of us spoke but each knew the other was acknowledging the personal nature of the battle. Standing there in that dark room I knew that I almost had the problem solved. And the witch knew it. She inclined her head in my direction, closed her eyes. She could rest now the bulldozer had departed. Granny shrank to being just another tired old woman.

# 18

The crowds converged on Town Park; the hot, heavy dusk shepherding them toward the lights, the excitement. Holidaymakers and natives jostled for the best view of the fire and fireworks. For most of them tonight marked the end of Carnival Week. They had no role and no interest in the official luncheon and presentations arranged for tomorrow; last rites for the dying carnival. Bonfire night was the finale of the week. For some it was a last chance to drink away the failures of the week, to drown regrets for lost opportunities. For others the burden was of opportunities taken. The number of tight-lipped landladies bearing unpaid bills would be more than equalled by the worried girls writing down faked addresses offered by sullen young men.

Such entertaining facts brought me no

comfort sitting legless on a park bench. Something in my attitude or in my face must have been exceptionally repellent because I had the bench to myself in the middle of the swirling crowd. My only need was met — to sit still, blank-eyed, empty-headed — an exhausted carcase struggling to breathe through its skin. I felt the weight of approaching night bearing down, dragging my eyelids down over my eyeballs — making a death mask.

I shifted uneasily on the seat. Tremayne's death mask. Knowing the body had always been in police custody had not entirely eliminated wishful thinking that it might be a lead. Further enquiries by my colleagues had established that the mask had been made three yeas ago as a kind of joke at a charity sale. The coincidence of the date had been seized on at once, but some of my colleagues had been slower to see the possibility of a link between Rymer and a certain Mr Rimmer who, according to Mrs Tremayne, had made the mask.

Reluctantly, I sidled into the festering,

noisy crowd, acknowledging more reasons for wanting rain. A lot of bodies needed cleansing and cooling. Slowly, I worked my way forward, seeking a good view of the presentation of prizes for the carnival guy competition. A hand gripped my elbow. I half-turned, the angry words rising. I was silenced by the expression on her face.

'Yes,' she said. 'Here's another tired detective.'

'We've nothing else in common,' I snapped, as Green threaded her arm through mine, insisted on walking beside me despite the crowd.

'Randy Jack Bull,' she said, softly. 'Hard man — and fool! You know in your heart, wherever that is, the difference between acts of love and acts of duty.'

I wanted to accept the hint, wanted only a proof I had misjudged her in the hot moment, in the rage I had felt at Frimmer's barbaric intrusion into my life. As if feeling my response through my arm, she pressed closer. I was cheered that my bodily responses to her suggestiveness were unaffected by scalds or exhaustion. How pleasant to be insatiable. How unfortunate I loathed her!

Near the front of the crowd we stopped and waited. I cursed my lack of height. For some reason I felt it was important to see if Granny Hemyock got a prize. The guys were propped up in a long row before the huge pyre. Their heads lolled, limbs spidered across the grass. Although they were all dead their glass eyes glittered knowingly in the floodlights. But none of them looked like Tremayne. I wondered if Granny Hemyock had decided not to enter. What that might prove I did not know.

The mayor arrived looking like a particularly unkempt guy. Speeches were made, prizes announced. The crowd grew restive. They wanted fire. The guys were hoisted to their appropriate levels on the pyre, the winner at the top. A Mrs Hemyock was second, came forward sulkily to accept the inferior prize, cast spiteful looks at the innocent cleric whose youth club entry had won. A young girl, prettier than Anna Duras, stepped to the edge of the pyre and ignited it with a taper. She jumped nervously as the lights were switched off and the first fireworks exploded overhead. The flames rushed upward round Tremayne's effigy. How unlike him it was. But if it could have spoken just once before the rising fire licked it into everlasting silence? I looked at Granny Hemyock leaning on her stick.

In that moment of fire rush, crowd cheer, firework glory, I solved the case. I solved it partly because I realized what had been missing at the cottage. In that instant so much fell into place. How often police work is like that: none of the puzzle done because one piece is missing, then as that piece is found all the others jump madly to their places. But one of the pieces made me feel sick. I had actually seen an abduction take place and had not realized the fact. So simple, so obvious and it had not registered with me until now. All the excuses, all the reasons flooded into my mind, but they would never be enough to supply all the self-justification I needed.

'Susie — ' I stopped short. Like a rocket bursting came the knowledge now was not the moment. I had to lock *every* piece in place before daring to present the picture to my colleagues. My failure to recognize the vital piece might then be less glaringly obvious. Several confirmations were needed. Green looked at me questioningly. 'Let's go,' I said, weakly.

We forced a path through the crowd and entered a zone of subdued light, prone bodies, bulging passions. As we picked our way between the lovers Green unwittingly provided me with some of that desperately needed confirmation.

'I wonder if your friend Rymer is here?' she said, jokingly.

'Not he,' I said, curtly.

'Not with his girl?' she asked. 'What's the matter?'

'His girl?' I stood still, looking at her.

'Well — I thought so. They were very passionate together the night of the parade. What *is* wrong?'

'You read his file?' I asked, gently.

'Yes. Why?'

'Because Rymer is a bloody raging queer, a queen, a pouf, bent as a boomerang!'

'But there's nothing on his record. I thought he walked like that because you broke his leg!'

'Jesus Christ!'

'What does — ?'

'It means that the last thing he'd have is a girl.'

'So?'

'So I won't see much of my bed tonight, either. There's work to do.'

# 19

The Operations Room was stifling. It contained too many worried men. Now that I had finished speaking I knew I could not stay awake much longer.

'Gentlemen, the Chief Constable and I will be interested in any coments you have to offer on what DC Bull has said.' Shalvin waited, his slightly horsy face damp with perspiration.

'Surprising!' said Cloag, nastily. 'Very surprising that only now have you got round to putting these ideas together. I seem to recollect you were collating reports for me as long ago as last Sunday. It's taken you a remarkably long time to develop this theory that Rymer was passing girls onto the Hemyock people.'

'Yes, sir,' I said, stolidly, in my best yokel constable manner. Once again Cloag was getting close to a target without quite identifying it. At this stage I had no intention of admitting to Cloag, or to anyone else, that I had actually seen the abduction take place. I had seen six Revellers in Cross Street and had seen six of them dancing when they got round the corner. The fact that with six dancers there must have been someone else in the wheelchair was something I'd missed at the time. Ironically, if I'd stuck to my assigned position I would have missed it anyway.

'I think,' said Shalvin, 'that experienced officers recognize the problems in such situations. For example, none of us — at the time — thought to follow up *in detail* all the references to the man Rymer. Everyone who saw him, including DS Green here, saw him at the same point along the route and merely reported the fact. It is only now, days later, and thanks largely to DC Bull that we can see the possibilities in those sightings. Bull followed up the reports last night and established that PCs Buttle and Piper saw Rymer standing at the kerbside alone whereas Detective Sergeant Green saw him in a shop doorway with a girl. Not knowing he is a homosexual, and there's never been a case brought against him so there's nothing on his record, she did not mention that detail. After all the street was full of couples petting.'

'But knowing the nature of the case — ' protested Cloag, determined to make trouble for someone.

'But we all knew the nature of the case,' said Shalvin, sharply, 'and for that very reason most of us would not have considered Rymer. Hindsight makes us appear more stupid than we are.'

'And less observant,' said the Chief Constable. 'Bull did not see Rymer at all.'

'In that crowd — ' I said.

'Merely an observation on my part,' lied Slinfield, smoothly.

'What worries me,' said Sergeant Bone, 'is that having listened to Bull's theory I see no way of proving it. Let me finish!' He scowled at Green who bit on her lip. I would never know if she had meant to defend me. 'The theory is,' said Bone, firmly, 'that Rymer picked up a girl he'd had his eye on and fed her some kind of drug. She was then responsive to the suggestion of taking a ride in Granny Hemyock's wheelchair as part of the fun. As a result she was abducted unprotesting in full view of the crowd but on part of the route not covered by one of our men. No one in the crowd thought anything odd about it. It was just carnival high jinks. The fact that no wheelchair was seen yesterday is apparently support for this theory, although no one can tell us why she was abducted. It is also suggested, that as a result of a tip-off Granny got rid of the chair, possibly over the cliff, because it was blood-stained. Of course, it may not be blood-stained and may have been in the sea for some time now. I appreciate Jack's 'feeling' about this case but I'm worried as to what we gain even if we *do* find a wrecked wheelchair in the sea. If Bull is correct and Granny is unbalanced then finding her wheelchair may not wring information out of her.'

'I agree,' said Chief Inspector Richardson, tugging at his uniform tie. He felt uncomfortable for many reasons, not only because he was a stranger in our midst.

I guessed that his worst suspicions about his crazy Clapton colleagues were being confirmed. 'What will you do if this Hemyock woman comes up with some other explanation of how and why she lost her wheelchair over the cliff?'

'Can I coment here, sir?' I paused only long enough for Shalvin to nod his head. 'I believe that Granny Hemyock will *never* confess to anything. I think it likely that even if we had an absolutely watertight case she would simply relapse into silence. We cannot regard her as the only target. We need a version of the domino theory. I mean we pick off the weaker brethren first in the hope of collapsing the whole gang through mutual recrimination and incrimination. The reason why I think this would work is that Snoad, Greening and Block were absolutely horrified at what Granny had done with that guy. She probably persuaded her girl to drag it into the bus for her, but for the others the whole episode was a nasty shock. Don't forget that, as far as we knew, they are only petty villains.

However tight her hold on them her own crazy behaviour is undermining it. Perhaps guilt by association — association in the abduction and murder of young women — will fail as her method of control.'

'You think that incident with the guy was a kind of boasting; like the bare-faced method of kidnapping?' prompted Shalvin.

'Yes, sir. We all know how criminals love to brag. That's how we catch some of 'em. For someone unbalanced the bragging may take an extreme form. No sane person would kidnap a girl in so public a fashion even though the victim had already been softened up for them.'

'Even so it does have a peculiar sort of camouflage about it', said Richardson. 'Er — what I mean is, such unlikely behaviour is itself a kind of front or blind, especially on Carnival Night when odd behaviour is all part of the fun.' To the man's relief some of us nodded. Perhaps we were in the same Force as himself after all.

'Yes, well,' said Shalvin. He looked questioningly at Dan Thirkettle, the only person present who had not spoken. Dan said nothing, crouched deeper in his chair. That slight body movement was more distressing to me than any comment might have been. I wanted Dan to act in a way that made nonsense of my suspicions. It would be so easy for him to do so. After all, there were no facts to go on. If there was a traitor present I nursed the hope it would prove to be Cloag.

'The Chief Constable will now outline this morning's operations,' said Shalvin.

'Lady and gentlemen,' said Slinfield, 'while most of you have been enjoying your sleep, Detective Chief Superintendent Shalvin, DS Green and myself have been drawing up a plan of operations. Also involved was DC Bull who took his bright idea, if I may call it that, to Detective Chief Superintendent Shalvin who immediately contacted me. Until I inform you of our plans only the four persons just named know precisely what they are. Being aware of the unpleasant possibility that the Hemyock people were tipped off yesterday, and perhaps on occasions in the past, you will appreciate the point of my remarks. There is a connection between this unfortunate situation and the presence here of Chief Inspector Richardson from Harmsworth. He is as unhappy about the reason for his involvement as I am. However, most of you know him by reputation if not by sight, and you know he will carry out his duties absolutely impartially.'

Slinfield paused, picked up a sheet of paper from the table. I thought the opening remarks and pause quite effective. Maybe the old sod was getting better at dealing with people. As though responding to my thoughts he decided to stand up for the rest of the briefing. With the windows behind him, his shadow was ominously long across the table.

'I do not apologize for what I now have to say,' said Slinfield, forcefully. 'My Force has an enviable reputation and I will not have that reputation besmirched by this deplorable case.

'One. It is now 06.20 hours — I am not apologizing for that either — and the operations we are about to launch will be concluded by 08.30 hours. This will be

241

possible because Shalvin and Richardson have already briefed almost everyone else involved, but in such a way that the particular targets have not yet been named. For example, Sergeant Bradninch and two of Richardson's men are standing by to arrest a particular villain. They do not yet know who their man is, nor do they know how their job fits into the overall pattern. Of course, we cannot conceal that something big is laid on but we can hide our specific aims.

'Point two relates to my previous point. Every group of officers from Clapton will be accompanied by officers under Chief Inspector Richardson's control. There will be no exceptions to this. My reference to Sergeant Bradninch was therefore purely illustrative. No one doubts *that* officer's loyalty.' He accompanied this platitude with a hard look at Green. The sower of mistrust inspected her bust. 'To keep control of security I have given orders that no telephone call may be made from this station or any other in the county until after 08.30 hours. Furthermore, the public telephone system is receiving the maximum scrutiny I can legally arrange. I made the last outgoing call from here some time before this meeting began. I confirmed my request for assistance from Scotland Yard. That was on *my* personal initiative and without reference to DS Green.

'That decision is point three, namely that this operation is our last independent operation in the case of the missing girls.

'Gentlemen, your faces betray you. I understand how you feel after all your efforts, not least your efforts in the last few days. But the situation is now very serious. Although we now have three bodies in the mortuary the bodies of three missing girls have not been found. The Tremayne lead seems to have petered out and provided us with no useful evidence relating *directly* to the disappearances. After three years of effort and the kidnapping of four girls we are at the end of Carnival Week once again, and all we have as a basis for further action is this very flimsy, unsupported theory from DC Bull.'

Once again I was coldly scrutinized. I

was not sure whether I was glad or sorry that Jones and Piper had seen nothing! But their car had been round the corner out of view at the crucial moment; the moment when I had disobeyed orders and crawled across that sticky roof. And afterwards, with dancers between them and the chair, my colleagues had not noticed anything odd about the passenger in the wheelchair. And if they had would they have remarked on it, on crazy, happy Carnival Night? Then, before the end of the procession route was reached, the Revellers had turned off along a side alley just as they had done every other year. One result of that had been that they had not appeared on the TV coverage of the ending of the parade. Slinfield rapped on the table.

'At 06.45 hours Rymer will be arrested by Bradninch and his men. At the same moment a number of other arrests will be made, other people invited to assist us with our inquiries. I confidently expect several useful spin-offs from this operation.

'The aim is to bring in every person

known to be or suspected to be involved criminally with Granny Hemyock. This aim will be achieved in such a way that communication between these persons will be nil. I repeat, will be nil. Interrogation of suspects will commence at 09.30 hours whether the Yard team has arrived or not.

'Everyone in this room will be directly involved in the swoop on Granny Hemyock's cottage. They will be assisted by fourteen uniformed constables who have come from Harmsworth with the Chief Inspector. The primary aim is to detain everyone there and keep them separated from each other. In the event of any legalistic argument we are claiming that some of the scrap metal we turned over yesterday is believed to be stolen. When you bring them back here you will find that, because of the shortage of cells, some other accommodation is being used as well. Any suspect placed in an ordinary room will always, always be accompanied by two constables.

'A small group will approach the cottage by the cliff path. That group will consist of six men including Sergeant Bone and Detective Sergeant Thirkettle. The four constables with you come from Harmsworth. DS Thirkettle — you are in charge in the field. You are to ensure that your patry inspects the beach at the bottom of that cliff for any signs of a wheelchair or anything else that might have a bearing on the case. You will approach the beach along the cliff-foot path from Clapton. Fortunately, the state of the tide is absolutely right in the next hour or so. You will then climb the cliff path and approach the cottage from the south-west side. This will seal off that route should anyone attempt to escape from the main party. You will arrive at the clifftop just before 08.15 hours. At 08.15 hours precisely all groups, including yours, will converge on the cottage. I will repeat that time: 08.15 hours.

'The main group will approach the cottage by cars along the track or else by walking through the woods. It will be led by Detective Chief Superintendent Shalvin and will include everyone else in this room except myself. I will remain here in charge of the Operations Room and ready to receive the team from the Yard. The Ops Room staff are waiting outside now and their numbers have been increased by two sergeants from Harmsworth. The Chief Superintendent will now brief his party in the CID room. Sergeants Bone and Thirkettle remain here with me until the Ops Room team has settled back in here. Any questions?

'Right. I must stress that holding these people incommunicado is vital. No two in the same car, same cell, same anything. Our hopes may be dim, our methods need not be. The time, gentlemen — and lady — is exactly 06.32 hours. At 08.15 hours you will meet together again at Granny Hemyock's cottage. Good luck!'

# 20

I leaned against a tree and looked out from the wood to Granny Hemyock's cottage. The heat was already stifling. The storm that had not broken yesterday was now standing overhead in black-bellied clouds. All the distant sky was dirty yellow. Nothing moved except a spiral of smoke from the cottage chimney. It climbed slowly, almost stiffly through the humid air. Only a mad woman would light a fire today.

Green was leaning on the other side of the tree trunk. Between our sagging bodies the tree was held vertical against the weight of the clouds. 'How much longer?' she whispered, without turning her head.

'Five minutes,' I said. My stomach lurched as if I had been drinking Granny's tea. Five minutes to finding out if I'd made a complete fool of myself. How could Granny dance at her age, with her bad leg? Could I swear to the truth of my recollection that *six* figures had been dancing round a loaded wheelchair? If the mind is dimmed by grief, exhaustion, desperation, what kind of distorted pictures does it project into our consciousness? The pictures we need to see, most want to see? Had I been alone, had time, I might have calmed myself sufficiently to project the pictures again, to redevelop and reprint my memory, as it were. But there was no time and Green had not left my side since the briefing. Frimmer's faithful bitch!

There were other problems. Rymer had been missing from his home when Bradninch burst in. But we had found his car on the top road above the woods. I had let down the rear tyres and Green had jammed hairpins in the locks. Despite these precautions I remained uneasy. The thought of Rymer waiting in the cottage with Granny — . Who was it who had said to me: 'Don't ever think you've got anyone in your pocket'? If my theory about kidnapping was right then Rymer had been laughing at me, at all of us, for years. He had amply repaid us for sending him down.

'Wonder how things are going on the cliff path?' Green's words lanced through my thoughts.

'Up and down,' I said, childishly. 'You should've gone with them.' I did not want reminding of the scale of the operation I had initiated.

'But I'd be away from you. Mr Frimmer likes us to stay together, to be close.'

'Not too close,' I said, jerking my thumb over my shoulder. Twenty yards behind us, lurking like a dirty wish, were our two escorting constables from Harmsworth. 'I'm as suspect as the rest.'

'Of course. What did you expect? Only you and I *know* you're straight — and that's why we're suspicious of Dan. You're just as suspect as far as Richardson and company are concerned.'

'You needn't've said that. And I *know* this could be my last mistake.'

'Pessimist,' she said, softly. 'You've

managed to convince enough people already, and none of them are fools.'

'Mebbe. But we're easily convinced when we want to be. I reckon I could've sold any story at that briefing.'

'Perhaps. But I've a feeling the truth will turn out even stranger than you've suggested. But don't worry. If the axe falls it will strike us all quite impartially.'

'Thanks.'

'Nearly time.' A tiny figure appeared on the clifftop skyline beyond the cottage.

'I think it's Bone,' I said. 'He's waving. Don't know why he's doing that. Thirty seconds to go. One of the Harmsworth PCs has joined him. Twenty seconds.' I paused. 'No sign of Dan yet. Ready? Go!'

We walked out under the black clouds. There were movements in the woods nearby as the general advance began. Down the track cars started up. A quarter of the way to the cottage there was no sign our approach had been observed. Halfway, everything quiet. Then, a few yards from the gate, the sky roared down drenching us before we could run. Cursing the rain, not knowing it was to save my life, I staggered up to the gate and, foolishly ignoring the broken fence on each side, held it open for Green. We huddled together under the porch, almost glad it was our job to get there first. It was impossible to see or hear any of our colleagues through the rain. Perhaps they weren't coming.

'Hansel and Gretel are back again,' said Green.

'Get in!' I snapped, slamming my shoulder against the door.

As we burst in, the building shook with the first clap of thunder. Green ran straight to Granny Hemyock's sitting-room. I turned left and threw open the kitchen door.

In that dark, greasy, cavernous room the occupants appeared literally thunder-struck. Granny Hemyock, who had been stirring a great pot over the fire, sat motionless, ladle suspended from her hand. Her minions were all present: Snoad, Greening, Block still in pyjamas, the girl vacant-faced as ever, and Pete Rymer; all struck dumb by my spectacular entry on the crest of the storm. Even Rymer.

'Morning,' I said, weakly. Suddenly I needed Green very badly.

Then the young girl began swearing in a monotonous filthy chant.

'Quiet Grace!' snapped Granny. Grace! The inappropriateness of the name. But my momentary advantage had gone. Rymer pushed himself up out of his chair, put his hand in his pocket, stepped toward me. And I had chosen not to be armed!

'No!' said Granny. Rymer stood still.

'You didn't think I came alone, did you?' I was finding it difficult to speak.

'Come here, young Bull,' said Granny.

I walked unsteadily toward her and the appalling heat of that fire. I knew I was safer with my back to the door, hoped and prayed colleagues were ready and waiting. I stood beside her. The fire began eating at my rain-soaked clothes, my sweating body. There was an abrupt movement behind me. I looked over my shoulder. Rymer had moved to the door, was standing with his back against it. He began cleaning his fingernails with a very sharp knife.

'Excuse his manners,' said Granny,

softly. 'And excuse me cooking. Mutton stew. My boys are hungry, always hungry.' She cackled harshly, stirring the stinking, bubbling mass. 'You haven't come here to taste my stew.'

'No, Granny. We've come for — '

'We've come? Why don't you call in your lady friend?'

Lightning lit the room. A tremendous clap of thunder rocked the cottage, shook soot down the chimney into the stew, made Block curse and drop the newspaper previously frozen in his great fists. The door burst open. Rymer was hurled across the room onto Snoad's knees. Green stood in the doorway, pale-faced, hand in handbag. I shook my head. Rymer stood up cursing. He had sliced the top off his left thumb. Blood spattered the floor, the man's clothes.

'You all right, Bull?' demanded Green, tensely. Behind her, uniformed men were entering the cottage. Rain lashed into the hall. I nodded, turned back to Granny.

'Granny, Granny,' I whispered, 'we've come about the girls again, the missing girls.'

'Not here and you know so,' she said, equally softly. Our conversation was overheard only by the fire, hissing as it consumed the rain in the chimney. Everyone else was watching Green in the doorway.

'Granny, your chair's missing too. The chair you used to carry them away.' I rested my hands against the smoke-stained bricks of the chimney breast, leaned down over the old woman. She knew she had lost.

'Did they have grey eyes, young Bull. grey eyes?' I felt as if I was being pulled down into her mad face.

'Some did, I think. Not sure of all.'

'Look!' she commanded. She stirred the pot, dug deep. A single grey eye floated across the bubbling surface.

With one heaving rush I vomited into the pot. Something struck the back of my head. I fell against Granny, carried her with me, under me, down into the great fire-place. As I lost consciousness I heard her beginning to scream, heard a shot.

# 21

I struggled against asphyxiating sensa-
tions: breath-taking pain tearing at my
right side, the choking stench of vomit,
raw hammer blows of heavy rain against
my face. I could smell the rain and the
damp earth but those scents did not mask
the disgusting smell of burnt flesh. I
wondered if I was dying. Opening my
eyes I discovered I was lying on the
ground, head propped on something soft.
A forest of legs surrounded me. Protec-
tively? I tried to move and the world was
red.

'Lie still, Jack. You're a bit scorched.'

The speaker was a fool. I was more
than scorched. And why did the back of
my head ache so much? And why did the
legs round me move backward and
forward in a rhythmic fashion? I twisted
my head sideways and nearly put out my

eye on Green's left nipple. That explained the soft pillow. Perhaps it explained the movements of the legs. Her heavy breathing was pushing my head forward, then letting it fall back. But there was no chance to enjoy it. There was something I had to find out. I forced away the restraining arms, clutched at shoulders, pulled myself upright.

'Granny?' I bleated.

'Dead,' said Green, bluntly. 'God knows what was in that stewpot but as you two knocked it into the fire it went up like a petrol bomb. By the time I'd dragged you off her it was too late. You only survived because your clothes were wringing wet from this cloudburst.'

'But the others?'

'We got 'em all.'

'No. no! Didn't they help with Granny?'

'No. And *I* was more concerned about *you* than about her. I had to shoot Block in the leg when he tried to throw a second log at you. Rymer was too busy holding his thumb to help anyone, and the other three rushed out screaming something about the roof. Cloag and party grabbed them.'

'That thing's Granny?' I pointed at the stained and reeking heap of rags nearby, ineffectually draped with a dirty table cloth.

'Yes. 'Fraid so.'

I squinted at the charred mound. My adversary was dead like Tremayne. Like Tremayne, dead without confirming or disproving our suspicions.

'You take it easy, Jack.' Shalvin, fuzzy at the edges, wobbled into my line of sight. 'The ambulance is coming.'

'Yes, sir. What's happening?' I did not care all that much but some vestige of discipline or self-preservation compelled the question.

'We're trying to stop the fire spreading but the thatch has caught and we've only a few buckets and the garden pump. I've sent for the brigade but I'm not sure they can get right up here. Maybe this bloody rain'll help damp it down. Excuse me, son.'

Most of my colleagues were engaged in the slightly ridiculous task of standing in drenching rain while passing buckets of water from hand to hand. Others stood guard over the prisoners. Block was sitting with his back against the wing of a police car while two constables strapped his leg. Rymer was having his hand bandaged by PC Aplin while another constable stood by, awkwardly holding Rymer's knife as though it was a truncheon. Thick white smoke billowed from the cottage. Driving rain, lightning flashes, the yellow-grey light, gave the scene a macabre air. The noise and confusion seemed to be contained in my skull. I staggered, felt Green's supporting arm at my waist, then gasped in agony as her hand brushed against my burnt right side. I leaned heavily against her.

'We started and finished with me getting burnt, eh, Susie?'

I wondered why I kept on talking when it was so painful. But there was something to say, to ask. I remembered the eye Granny had spooned up for me to see. As though in mockery klaxons began to blare. The fire brigade was arriving too late to save the breakfast. Vomit rose again through my mouth and nostrils. As I fainted again I felt Green quivering with disgust.

My mind was behaving like a small child dipping in and out of a forbidden pool. Return to consciousness was swift. I heard the Fire Chief ordering his men to tear the smoking thatch off the cottage. I felt the collective shock at this instruction, recognized the shock was in Granny Hemyock's thugs. Only Rymer did not care about the roof coming off. He was more interested in the work of the man bandaging his thumb for him. The others stood between their unsuspecting guards and stared in horror at their burning home. The intensity of their regard could not be explained by the excitement of the race between the roof being heated from below and soaked by rain from above. I struggled to my feet once more, despite curses from Green.

The fire engine was jammed between the gate posts on the track. Firemen were running up the slope from it carrying ladders. The first fireman on the roof hacked loose a great divot of new thatch.

It slid hesitantly down the eave, plunged smouldering into the front garden. A policeman stepped forward with a bucket of water. A terrible cry from the roof sent him scuttling back to safety, spilling his bucket. Startled faces turned up to the fireman who had cried out. A second bundle had been cut free and was beginning to slither down the sagging, smoking roof. Every eye refocused on the sliding mass: not thatch but a polythene wrapped, part-cooked selection of human remains. The ghastly package smashed onto the ground, split apart and disgorged the dismembered naked torso and limbs of a young woman. They lay spread like a dissected, sun-bleached starfish. There was no head.

'Get the whole roof off!' bellowed Shalvin. 'Burning or not — get it down!'

More firemen climbed ladders, tore at the thatch, hurled down other gruesome packages. And all the time above the storm, the voices, the swearing of the girl, I could hear someone being dreadfully sick. This time it wasn't me.

'Susie,' I groaned. 'Get me to Rymer.

Don't argue! Just lend me your shoulder!'

Rymer saw us coming and half-limped, half-trotted to meet us. PC Aplin, holding the end of the bandage, was obliged to follow. Rymer halted two paces away, looked beseechingly from face to face.

'I didn't cut 'em, Bull! Granny did it all. The old bitch did it all. I only found out last night. That's why I came up here this morning. Honest to God!'

'But you helped.'

'She made me. She put the finger on 'em. Told me which one to pick up each time. I thought they were for her sex parties, that black magic shit. I swear that's the truth! I wouldn't've touched them girls if I'd known she was choppin' 'em. She said they were for parties. She'll tell. You make her tell — she'll tell!'

'But she won't. She's dead. Reckon I've got you along with the rest. You'll not wriggle out from under this one. And how many bodies d'you think we'll find here? Three? And there was one on the building site. Bet you know all about that!'

A dark stain appeared on the front of Rymer's trousers. Grey-faced, his eyes rolling upward, he slumped back against Aplin's ample chest.

'Watch him,' I said. 'He's bloody dangerous and he knows he's in this up to his neck.'

I turned round, turning Green with me. I wanted to find out what Shalvin was doing. The Chief Superintendent was yelling into his car radio; his voice almost happy. He was sending messages for the Chief Constable, Crime Squad Regional Co-ordinator, Chief Superintendent Admin., pathologist, lab officer, photographers, everybody. Everybody. This was the climax of his career and no one, nothing was going wrong this time. After three barren years of unrewarded painstaking routine, of cheap jibes, hard words, he was making sure everything happened and happened fast. As if to emphasize his triumph another package came tumbling off the shattered roof.

We walked slowly toward him. Then beyond him we saw a line of cars forming behind the fire engine. The Chief Constable was arriving with the party from Scotland Yard. 'They're just too late,' said Green, in my ear.

'Who are?' asked Shalvin. Then, following the direction of Green's pointing hand, he turned and saw the Chief Constable climbing from the first car. 'Bloody marvellous,' he said. 'And not too late. Just on time to offer their congratulations to me. And to you, Green. Your boss is down there as well. As for you, Jack, looks like you came good on the last lap. All we need now is that wheelchair with fingerprints and/or bloodstains. But even without it I think this gang'll crack now.'

'Bone's taking his time,' said Green.

'Yes,' said Shalvin. 'He went back again for something but there he is now. No sign of the wheelchair though, nor Thirkettle. You can see the Harmsworth PCs just coming up over the cliff edge. Dan's bringing up the rear, I expect. Not as young as he was.

'But you must go off to hospital, son. Don't wait around here any longer. Your Mr Frimmer don't want damaged goods.'

But I was staring past Shalvin, past a gesticulating Sergeant Bone, past the four constables. I was staring at the cliff edge.

# 22

'Sir! Sir!' cried Bone, while still twenty yards away. Lack of self-possession in a man so self-possessed confirmed my fears even before he broke the news. 'It's — it's Dan Thirkettle. He's dead!'

'How?' cried Shalvin, leaning against the car door. The rain made a hollow, drumming noise on the roof. Bone took a deep breath, steadied himself.

'He slipped when halfway up the cliff path. He decided to come up last and insisted on carrying the wheelchair himself, said it was CID evidence. No one had a chance to help him when he fell. I'd already reached the top of the cliff when it happened. That right?' He appealed to the four white-faced constables as they arrived beside him. They nodded, muttered their appalled agreement.

'And you left him?' I whispered.

'No!' said Bone, angrily. 'we went back down to the beach. He was — was obviously dead. I put my cape over him. Then we had to climb straight back up. We knew we were going to be late.'

'But what about the wheelchair?' snapped Green.

You miserable officious cow, I thought. Trust you to keep *your* mind on the job.

'That's down there as well,' said Bone, shortly. 'Enough blood on it to satisfy even you.' Green said nothing, raised her eyebrows. 'We should've brought it with us but I was more concerned not to be delayed any further. We'll get it when we go back down for Dan.'

'It was accidental — that he slipped?' Shalvin stared at Bone.

'That's what I'm reporting, sir,' said Bone, firmly. He had served with both Dan and Shalvin for many years.

'Agreed?' snapped Shalvin, looking at the Harmsworth constables. They all nodded. They were young but they were not silly.

'Granny Hemyock's dead as well,' said

Shalvin. Bone just nodded. He also recognized that one kind of case might be closed already. He looked round at the scene, wanted to ask questions, but merely commented on the Chief Constable's arrival.

Everyone except me turned to greet Sir Bertie's party. Drained of all feeling, I slumped against the car, looked back toward the cottage. I saw Rymer smash his fist into the face of the constable, grab his knife and lunge at PC Aplin. As the point of the blade drove into Aplin's stomach I felt the blow within myself revitalizing me. Cursing with anger and pain, I pushed myself upright and began to run. As Aplin fell Rymer ripped the knife clear of the body and limped toward the woods.

For a moment, two men running made no impression amid the noise and confusion of that battleground. Then, behind us, we heard the first voices raised in consternation and anger, the first shouted orders. But no following footsteps could be heard above the noise of the storm. Hunter and hunted were isolated from the main pack even before we reached the trees.

Within the dark wood I ran with my left arm across the front of my body, my right arm straight down by my side but not touching it. One blow from a low branch would cripple me for good, especially if it caught my burns. With every jerking step I felt as if burnt flesh was stripping itself further from the bone. I assumed that Rymer was just ahead of me but there was no point in listening for footsteps. So heavy was the rain that the whole wood crackled with a bombardment of gobbets and splashes of water. The voices of colleagues sounded louder; hardly surprising if they were overhauling me, outstripping my tottering progress.

I might have blundered on in the same direction until collapsing if I had not caught sight of something moving away to the right. I swerved toward it. The blood-soaked hand bandage must have come undone, caught on the branch and Rymer had not stopped to disentangle it. I ran along the track Rymer had found. If no one else came the same way I would have to face Rymer alone. My mind found nothing wrong in the assumption I would overhaul him. Perhaps I was assuming that having crippled him some years ago I could reasonably expect to catch him now.

With every torturing step an alarming sense of familiarity began to trouble me. I recognized individual trees, clumps, avenues; knew this part of the wood. By ill-chance we were following the track Green and I had used earlier in the reverse direction. Rymer would reach the top road where the cars were parked. Finding his own car disabled he might try to use Green's. It was locked but a car is easily broken into, easily started without a key. If he got too far ahead of me he might have time to swop vehicles. I tried to steady my breathing, to concentrate on moving my legs smoothly.

Twenty yards from the road those legs began to bow, my body tilted forward. Just short of the road I crashed to the ground, lay gasping on the saturated carpet of last year's leaves. I thought I could hear Jeannie urging me on. Perhaps

I slipped into unconsciousness for a few seconds. But almost at once I became aware of a new sound only partly drowned by the liquid noises of the rain. I lifted my head.

Directly in front of me stood Rymer's old green Ford. On the far side, the offside, the blood and rain-soaked figure of Rymer was wrestling with the car door. The noise I had heard was the haft of Rymer's knife being smashed against the window. His panic had allowed me to catch him. As I pushed myself up to a kneeling position Rymer gave up banging the glass and tried to jam the point of his knife under the edge of the quarter light. As he heaved on the blade the point snapped off and he stumbled backward. I stood, stepped forward. Rymer saw me, raised the shortened knife, it's broken end more terrifying than a sharp point. We glared at each other. Rymer spoke, snarled. I could not hear him.

Suddenly, there was shouting along the road. We both risked a quick glance at the group of figures emerging from the wood about eighty yards away. Rymer must have thought he could still get the car going in time. He seized the door handle and wrenched at it with all his strength. The futility of the act encouraged me to step down onto the road. I suppose we had both passed the limits of sense. With an animal scream Rymer kicked the car. I fell forward across the bonnet, could not stand upright.

For an instant we stared at each other, our faces almost touching. Then Rymer raised the knife, raised it up to the treetops, into the sky, out of my line of sight. I pawed at the slippery metal under me but found no purchase. Dumbly, I waited for the blow.

'Don't move!' It was Green's voice. We both looked at her: twenty yards away, rain-soaked, dirty, advancing more slowly now; breathing hard but the pistol rock steady. Figures behind her checked their approach, watched the three of us.

Rymer may have meant to strike at me as a last insane gesture, or he may have meant to put the knife down, or just to ease his over-extended arm. Whatever the intention he never had a chance to carry it out. As soon as his right arm began descending Green started shooting.

The bullets struck only inches in front of me as I lay across the bonnet. I saw Rymer jerk forward under the first impact low in his body, then rear up and back as the second shot tore into his chest. Something hot spattered against my face. Rymer's right arm swerved in a downward arc and the knife dug screeching into the car door. The body slumped out of my sight and down the side of the car.

After the shots I imagined an instant almost peaceful, only rain-filled. Then the rooks rose shrieking, men resumed running, Green came up to the car. I dragged myself round the bonnet, looked down on Rymer.

'Never mind him,' gasped Green. 'Are you all right?'

'Wait,' I said and fell down beside Rymer. He was still breathing and his eyes were open. He stared at me, our faces a foot apart.

'Got your girl. Should've got you — as well.'

'What do you mean?' I said, slowly. But

I was speaking to a dead man.

It did not matter. Just above the body my question had its answer. Rymer's knife had made a deep scar in the door panel. The green paint chipped off was scattered like leaves, the scraped metal glinted silver. And all round the scar, between the silver and green, was black. Black is not the undercoat for green.

'Know now — Jeannie,' I said.

'Don't talk, Jack,' said Green, kneeling, gently taking my face between her hands. 'Sure we know it all now. We'll tie it up without Rymer.'

'No,' I said, carefully. 'Not that. I know Rymer killed Jeannie.'

As the trees in the wood toppled toward me, blocking my sight with their darkness, the last thing I saw was Green's lovely face beginning to distort.

# 23

## Obituaries

The one life I had deliberately and skilfully extinguished reproached me only by absence. Henry John Bishop stayed away. (How calmly I had bent over him, turned his warm heavy head to face me.) Everybody else came.

Granny Hemyock sat silent at my bedside, rocking slowly on the chair, staring blankly into my face. Sometimes Snoad and Greening were with her and then there was bawdy humour and sniggering. But if Jeannie came to my bed at the same time as Granny then the old woman became tiresomely talkative. She and Jeannie bickered across my body while I sweated and tossed in agony.

In boring, embarrassed processions my colleagues came and went: Bone — newly promoted, Bradninch, Shalvin, Thirkettle, Cloag, Slinfield. The latter was full of remarks about duty well done, successful conclusions. He was moved on by Frimmer. Then Abraham Gretz appeared at my bedside, a bundle of Jewish gestures and jokes. But there was something wrong with him and I was too ill to work out what it was.

Green visited many times but always appeared as if through a sheet of frosted glass. And after each of her visits I was more depressed and wanted Jeannie more. But Jeannie was appearing less often.

On my worst day Green came and brought Mrs Thirkettle with her. The wife remarked that Dan had always spoken very highly of me. Something terrible happened. Whether it was a reality or something in my tormented mind I never knew. But between the tubes, drips and grafts a finger of horror was inserted, breaking open my wounds. The same day I was rushed to another hospital.

I returned to Harmsworth Hospital during a period of autumn gales. Sane and snug in my private room, the air on my face fuzzy from the central heating, I lay with the blankets up under my chin and listened to the wind and rain lashing the hospital gardens. The violence of the weather touched me directly only as a gentle rubbing and nudging through the walls — like the remembrances of pain.

An almond-eyed nurse materialized at the foot of the bed. At last I was sufficiently recovered for nurses to stand out of reach. 'A Mr Shalvin is here to see you. Do you feel up to it after your journey?'

'Up to anything,' I said, vulgarly. 'Send him in, ducky.' Shalvin appeared, sat beside the bed.

'Hello, sir.'

'Hello, Jack. No need for the sir — not since last Friday. I'm officially retired.' Shalvin sounded smug. 'I rang the hospital and they said you'd be back today. How did it go.'

'OK, sir. This time all the grafts worked. Bit like a patchwork quilt down my right side but it's healing. I shouldn't have to be moved away again.'

'Well, you sound happier and in your right mind! You gave us the hell of a fright, young Bull.'

'Can't say I knew much about that. The Doc was telling me the trouble was not just the severity of the burns but also that I was too exhausted to heal properly.'

'Not surprised. That last month we were all desperately overworked.'

'But it begins to look like a success.'

'Is that right, young Bull!' Shalvin was savage. 'All I know is that between Carnival Night at about 22.00 hours and Wednesday morning at 08.50 hours seven people died. And only one of them, Anna Duras, was not killed during police action. And two of the dead, Aplin and Thirkettle, were lifelong colleagues of mine. Is that success? Or is it the discovery that the slaughtering of young girls has been happening on a larger scale than we ever dreamed? Or maybe it's your poor bloody grass, Abraham Gretz, tied down in the psychiatric ward just along the corridor from you? It that success?'

'Whaddya mean about Abe?'

'That clever Mr Frimmer visited him, remember? Just to clear him of being implicated in any way, incidentally clearing your snow-white name at the same time? We'll never know what was said but in one interview he broke that poor Jew more effectively than the Nazis could manage in six years.'

My mouth was very dry.

'Of course, you wouldn't've known; being incapacitated yourself.' Shalvin veered very, very slightly toward the apologetic.

'And Judith?' I asked, sharply.

'Oh, her! That really is success, Jack. Last I heard Frimmer had established her in a London flat.'

There was a long silence. I thought of other griefs.

'The inquests went all right?' I said. Shalvin knew exactly what I meant.

'Yes. Dan's was accidental death — like Granny Hemyock's.' We both contemplated the foot of my bed. 'Saw Mrs Thirkettle last week: good soul, coping well. The pension's safe. Block and company knew Granny had a policeman in her pocket but not who it was.'

'And if it *wasn't* Dan?'

'I've thought about that but I'm also retired. And why start another investigation based only on vague theories, especially as it might backfire and damage Dan's family in some way?'

We looked at each other, knowing that rotten apples can only deteriorate. It would be better for all of us if Dan had been proved guilty. Full circle, I thought. I turned our talk away from that subject.

'The Tremayne verdict was suicide?'

'Yes, Jack. And the Press made some joy out of Green being there. But at least we now know why he did it. He was being blackmailed by Granny.'

'He was?'

'Yeah. Granny let him know that his wife was mixed up in black magic, maybe hinted she was involved with the disappearing girls, including their own *au pair*.'

'But was she?'

'Well — yes and no. It was all so silly. She was only dabbling as were half the bored housewives in Clapton. Nothing criminal at all and certainly nothing to do with the girls. But of course, she felt tainted, and unwittingly fed Tremayne's suspicions by acting guilty when he tried to open up the subject.'

'You might almost say he died because they couldn't talk to each other?'

'Yeah. Both fed on suspicion and mistrust. He paid up when she wasn't really guilty of anything criminal.'

'That might explain his last remark: 'all about women'?'

'It might. There's a helluva lot we'll never explain.'

'Granny's lot all pleading guilty?'

'Except the girl — she's unfit to plead. Otherwise, they've been so co-operative it's almost indecent. We can't bring any murder charges. The juries will hear so much about Granny keeping them drugged and leading them on.'

'I suppose that's right.'

'But interestingly enough, only up to a point. Did you guess Granny was probably going to be the next victim?

'How come?'

'Well, her gang was loyal because they were the inner circle, trapped as witnesses and accomplices in the worst black magic, the human sacrifices. But the rot set in when they understood, in their drug-fuddled minds, that she had gone quite mad. The final blow was not that nonsense with the guy but the fact that she slit Anna Duras's throat while the girl was still in the wheelchair; wouldn't wait for the usual ceremony back at the cottage. At that moment her gang was *not* yet full of home-made drugs so they were absolutely horrified.

'No one is saying but we suspect that was why Rymer was up there that Wednesday morning. Having driven that stolen van to the building site, dumped Anna Duras and abandoned Bishop to your mercy, he was supposed to get rid of Granny as well. Until Anna was so blatantly murdered Rymer probably believed Granny's story that she passed the girls on to a London brothel.'

I was appalled by the picture of that evil old woman surrounded by a closing circle of fear-crazed thugs. Perhaps that explained her apparent indifference to discovery. I must have seemed an insipid kind of threat. I pushed myself deeper into the warm bed.

'Of course,' said Shalvin, 'Granny was so busy drugging them all with her herbs and potions I doubt if they will ever be able to tell the truth as the courts understand the word. Much of the time reality and hallucination were interwoven. You should see the statements they've made!'

I wasn't sure I wanted to. When all the charges have been brought there is time for obviousness to be as ugly as it sounds, for hindsight to make one ashamed. We had underestimated a crazy old woman, some simple-minded villains and a crippled queer. I had done worse. I had seen a major crime committed and not recognized it. That failure had not only cost a young woman her life but, far worse, had led to six other deaths including two colleagues. And I had actually uttered the words 'black magic' while standing on that building site, Bishop's body at my feet. I just hoped I had not been delirious when visitors stood at my bedside.

'Why d'you think Granny did it, sir?'

'Because she enjoyed it, especially the

power it gave her over victims and followers alike. But I'm a simple copper. I expect the psychiatrists will wrap it up a bit.'

'And where did she hold her secret ceremonies?'

'In her back garden. So obvious when you know, ain't it? Now we know why her plants grew so well.' I saw again those enormous plants swaying over the path, plucking at Green's clothing. 'When we checked the garden we found no traces of bone or flesh but the lab thinks the soil has been enriched with some kind of ashes.' Shalvin paused for a moment. 'Just thinking about it makes me mad! Digging her garden, turning over all that junk, and we were never more than a hundred yards from the bodies. She really did have the cheek of the devil! A roof stuffed with carefully packaged and preserved human remains — and us thinking the roof was patched like that because she was poor!'

'And it's not plain sailing now we do know about the roof. I've heard you say so often that cases have neat endings only in cheap thrillers. Even so this one seems a bit much!'

'Yes,' said Shalvin, dryly. 'Three bits too much. Two legs and an arm to be precise.'

'Read that in the Press. So at least five girls've been murdered.'

'No, lad, worse than that. Both the legs are right legs.'

'Christ! And there's no clue who the other victims were?'

'Only a couple of them. Part of the trouble is we've no idea where all the missing bits are. We've had all kinds of difficulties allocating the parts for burial. Some of the bereaved have been mourning over coffins largely filled with sand. And there are still three heads missing! They're certainly nowhere on Granny's property and I'm pretty sure her cronies are telling the truth when they say they can't remember what happened. All those herbs in their food!'

'Food — ugh! God, was I relieved to hear that her pot really did contain mutton stew. That was a sheep's eye the old bitch showed me.'

'And that last silly stunt killed her.'

'Block still says he thought I was attacking her, and that's why he crowned me with a log?'

'Yes. But it won't do him any good. Mind you, I'd thump you if you were sick in my breakfast!' Neither of us smiled.

'Another interesting loose end, Jack, is the man in the red cape and hood. He was not Henry John Bishop. Granny never told the others who he was and they never saw him unmask. But they did see him at the same time as Bishop. They only knew he was male because he spoke to them. Fortunately, he joined them only for the procession.'

'Why 'fortunately', sir?'

'You are still under the weather! How would we feel if he'd also been at the human sacrifices and was now continuing to live quietly in Clapton?'

'You mean he'd start up the business again?'

'It's a possibility — and one we don't want lurking on our patch. We'd like to know who he is even though we've nothing to charge him with. Appearing in a procession is not a crime. Even watching *you* is not against the law.'

'Assuming it was the same person in that alley.'

'Another thing we'll never know. Another loose end.'

'I wonder why Granny invited him? First step to compromising him? Perhaps something like that has happened to other townspeople. We really know sod-all don't we, sir?'

'Ha! That's not unusual! We can only speculate. It's quite bizarre looking at our more respected brethren and wondering about them.'

'Bizarre,' I said, sleepily.

'Well,' he said, heartily, '*you* won't be bothered by the loose ends in Clapton. I've heard from Frimmer that you're accepting his offer.'

'Yes, sir. Not a lot to keep me here now. I know I put myself back in favour a bit right at the end but I'll not be missed.'

'And you'll not miss us for long. You'll soon settle. Just as I'll settle in retirement.' Shalvin stood up. 'You're getting tired and I must go. I'm taking the wife out so can't be late. No official excuses any more.' He hesitated for a moment. 'Just one thing I ought to mention. In case it worried you.'

'Yes, sir?'

'That time DS Green brought Dan's wife to see you.' Shalvin paused. I felt sick. 'You probably don't remember but — you blew your top about Dan, made a scene. Fortunately, Green was able to shut you up and convince her that you were too ill to know what you were saying. Right? Got it?'

'Yes, sir. Real little Miss Fixit, that woman.'

'On that I must take your word,' Shalvin was poker-faced. 'But don't be *too* begrudging with thanks. One of her fixes saved your self-centred little neck.' I took a deep breath but he beat me to the punch. 'Goodbye, lad. See you next week.'

Shalvin marched out of the room. As the door swung backward and forward I could see him talking to someone in the corridor. Then he poked his head back into the room. 'Another visitor for you.

Just bite on your spiteful tongue, and remember — you need rest, Randy!' He disappeared. A moment later the door opened very slowly.

★   ★   ★

The last time I had seen her clearly she had been rainsoaked, spattered with mud and my vomit, walking toward me, pistol raised in a two-handed grip. Later, her face had been closer but blurred. She had smelt of cordite. Now she was elegantly dressed in blue, wore a silver-blonde wig and carried a folder of papers instead of a pistol.

'Hello, Jack.' She was pale-faced, nervous.

'Sit down, Susie. I suppose I must now thank you formally for saving my life.'

'You don't *have* to,' she said. As she sat down an over-powering wave of scent made me catch my breath. 'Sorry,' she said. 'Isn't it silly. I had an accident with the scent bottle.' A long pause. 'Hansel and Gretel again,' she said, weakly. I could think of nothing to say. 'I'm so pleased to know you're getting better. You'll be out of here soon?'

'Soon.' In the uncomfortable silence that followed each wanted to touch the other. For quite different reasons neither of us stretched out a hand.

'Did you do anything about Rymer's last words?' she asked.

'No point. What's in a dying whisper? What help would it be to Jeannie to re-open the inquest and change the verdict to murder?'

'None.'

I closed my eyes again. How typical she should have plunged into that subject. I had nothing to say to her. There was not a way left by which she could manipulate me.

'Jack!' The pain in her voice was like a knife. I felt I had to show some mercy.

'Listen!' I raised myself on my elbow. 'Your crew chose to use just about every dirty little trick in the book. *You* set me up as only a woman like you could set me up. If that's the way you work that's it. There are more ways of snaring a rabbit than one. But the rabbit doesn't have to applaud the choice while he's in the pot. *You* could present the whole thing as a glamorous story. Build it up to the big scene where you save my life. But I don't read it that way! I read Dan, Bill Aplin, Tremayne, poor bloody Abe!' I fell back on the pillow and closed my eyes. I could not bear to face the real passionate reason for her visit. There was a long, long silence.

'There's nothing more to be said, then?' She spoke very quietly.

'End of story.'

'I'll leave these papers on your bedside table. They're from Frimmer. Congratulations!'

'Sufficient unto the day.'

'Goodbye, Jack.'

I did not watch her walk away but busied myself pulling the blankets back under my chin. I felt a faint tremor run through the bed as the gale nudged the hospital wall. And Gretel vanished into the storm. I did not expect us to meet again. Hansel never did believe in fairy stories!

Drowsily, I looked at the cover of the

file she had left on the bedside table. It was addressed to Detective Sergeant J. Bull. I grinned to myself. For a pushy young sod it *was* a kind of fairy-tale ending.

## THE END

We do hope that you have enjoyed reading this large print book.

Did you know that all of our titles are available for purchase?

We publish a wide range of high quality large print books including:

**Romances, Mysteries, Classics General Fiction Non Fiction and Westerns**

Special interest titles available in large print are:

**The Little Oxford Dictionary Music Book, Song Book Hymn Book, Service Book**

Also available from us courtesy of Oxford University Press:

**Young Readers' Dictionary (large print edition) Young Readers' Thesaurus (large print edition)**

For further information or a free brochure, please contact us at:

**Ulverscroft Large Print Books Ltd., The Green, Bradgate Road, Anstey, Leicester, LE7 7FU, England. Tel:** (00 44) **0116 236 4325 Fax:** (00 44) **0116 234 0205**

*Other titles in the*
*Linford Mystery Library:*

# THE GIRL HUNTERS

## Sydney J. Bounds

Doll Winters was a naïve teenager, who fantasised about being a film character. But when Gerald Dodd committed a brutal killing, she found herself starring in a real-life murder drama — as the star witness! And when Dodd tries to silence her, Doll turns for help to the famous private detective Simon Brand. Then a further terrifying attempt on her life forces her to go on the run. But can Brand find her before the killer can?

# CRIME MOST FOUL

## George Douglas

When a teenager attacks an old lady, her best friend, Detective Constable Sheldon, wants revenge. Chief Superintendent Bill Hallam of North Central Regional C.I.D. forbids Brenda Sheldon to get involved in the case. Ignoring the ban her investigation, aided by Dave Morgan, leads her to a drug racket in Deniston. The trail is obscure until Molly Bilton tries to help a man involved with the drug pushers, but finds the man murdered, and her own life in danger.

# THE GILDED KISS

## Douglas Enefer

It was the key to a most baffling exploit for Dale Shand, but a lot was to happen to him and the bewitching Linda Travers before he found it. For her, Shand leaves his new headquarters in Baker Street, London, to travel across Europe and back, where he follows a trail of murder and big-time art theft. In a high-octane adventure, he encounters a sinister Spaniard, a mysterious girl and a missing heir — all enmeshed in the tangled web.

# BIGFOOT

## Richard Hoyt

Private Detective John Denson and his partner, Willie Prettybird, are helping Russian scientist, Dr. Sonja Popoleyev, in her search for the legendary Bigfoot. And with big money at stake, they also have competition in their quest, including Alford and Elford Pollard, local bigfoot hunters. But Elford is murdered before the expedition has begun. Soon, the searchers scramble for traces of the creature. But the murderer isn't finished yet, and Denson and his party are on the endangered species list.